michelle Pope

10661688

Humor · Horror · and the
SUPERNATURAL

22 stories by SAKI
(H. H. MUNRO)

Cover design by Janet and Alex D'Amato

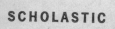

SCHOLASTIC **SBS** BOOK SERVICES

Published by Scholastic Book Services, a division
of Scholastic Magazines, Inc., New York, N. Y.

All rights reserved. This edition is published by Scholastic Book Services, a division of Scholastic Magazines, Inc., by arrangement with The Viking Press, Inc.

3rd printing . . . . January 1968

Printed in the U.S.A.

Contents

Gabriel-Ernest

"THERE is a wild beast in your woods," said the artist Cunningham, as he was being driven to the station. It was the only remark he had made during the drive, but as Van Cheele had talked incessantly his companion's silence had not been noticeable.

"A stray fox or two and some resident weasels. Nothing more formidable," said Van Cheele. The artist said nothing.

"What did you mean about a wild beast?" said Van Cheele later, when they were on the platform.

"Nothing. My imagination. Here is the train," said Cunningham.

That afternoon Van Cheele went for one of his frequent rambles through his woodland property. He had a stuffed bittern in his study, and knew the names of quite a number of wild flowers, so his aunt had possibly some justification in describing him as a great naturalist. At any rate, he was a great walker. It was his custom to take mental notes of everything he saw during his walks, not so much for the purpose of assisting contemporary science as to provide topics for conversation afterwards. When the bluebells began to show themselves in flower he made a point of informing everyone of the fact; the season of the year might have warned his hearers of the likelihood of such an occurrence, but at least they felt that he was being absolutely frank with them.

What Van Cheele saw on this particular afternoon was, however, something far removed from his ordinary range of experience. On a shelf of smooth stone overhanging a deep pool in the hollow of an oak coppice a boy of about sixteen lay asprawl, drying his wet brown limbs luxuriously in the sun. His wet hair, parted by a recent dive, lay close to his head, and his light-brown eyes, so light that there was an almost tigerish gleam in them, were turned towards Van Cheele with a certain lazy watchfulness. It was an unexpected apparition, and Van Cheele found himself engaged in the novel process of thinking before he spoke. Where on earth could this wild-looking boy hail from? The miller's wife had lost a child some two months ago, supposed to have been swept away by the millrace, but that had been a mere baby, not a half-grown lad.

"What are you doing there?" he demanded.

"Obviously, sunning myself," replied the boy.

"Where do you live?"

"Here, in these woods."

"You can't live in the woods," said Van Cheele.

"They are very nice woods," said the boy, with a touch of patronage in his voice.

"But where do you sleep at night?"

"I don't sleep at night; that's my busiest time."

Van Cheele began to have an irritated feeling that he was grappling with a problem that was eluding him.

"What do you feed on?" he asked.

"Flesh," said the boy, and he pronounced the word with slow relish, as though he were tasting it.

"Flesh! What flesh?"

"Since it interests you, rabbits, wild fowl, hares, poultry, lambs in their season, children when I can get any; they're usually too well locked in at night, when I do most of my hunting. It's quite two months since I tasted child flesh."

Ignoring the chaffing nature of the last remark, Van Cheele tried to draw the boy on the subject of possible poaching operations.

"You're talking rather through your hat when you speak of feeding on hares." (Considering the nature of the boy's toilet, the simile was hardly an apt one.) "Our hillside hares aren't easily caught."

"At night I hunt on four feet," was the somewhat cryptic response.

"I suppose you mean that you hunt with a dog?" hazarded Van Cheele.

The boy rolled slowly over on to his back, and laughed a weird low laugh that was pleasantly like a chuckle and disagreeably like a snarl.

"I don't fancy any dog would be very anxious for my company, especially at night."

Van Cheele began to feel that there was something positively uncanny about the strange-eyed, strange-tongued youngster.

"I can't have you staying in these woods," he declared authoritatively.

"I fancy you'd rather have me here than in your house," said the boy.

The prospect of this wild, nude animal in Van Cheele's primly ordered house was certainly an alarming one.

"If you don't go, I shall have to make you," said Van Cheele.

The boy turned like a flash, plunged into the pool, and in a moment had flung his wet and glistening body halfway up the bank where Van Cheele was standing. In an otter the movement would not have been remarkable; in a boy Van Cheele found it sufficiently startling. His foot slipped as he made an involuntary backward movement, and he found himself almost prostrate on the slippery weed-grown bank, with those tigerish yellow eyes not very far from his own. Almost instinctively he half raised his hand to his throat. The boy laughed again, a laugh in which the snarl had nearly driven out the chuckle, and then, with another of his astonishing lightning movements, plunged out of view into a yielding tangle of weed and fern.

"What an extraordinary wild animal!" said Van Cheele as he picked himself up. And then he recalled Cunningham's remark, "There is a wild beast in your woods."

Walking slowly homeward, Van Cheele began to turn over in his mind various local occurrences which might be traceable to the existence of this astonishing young savage.

Something had been thinning the game in the woods lately, poultry had been missing from the farms, hares were growing unaccountably scarcer, and complaints had reached him of lambs being carried off bodily from the hills. Was it possible that this wild boy was really hunting the countryside in company with some clever poacher dog? He had spoken of hunting "four-footed" by night, but then, again, he had hinted strangely at no dog caring to come near him, "especially at night." It was certainly puzzling. And then, as Van Cheele ran his mind over the various depredations that had been committed during the last month or two, he came suddenly to a dead stop, alike in his walk and his speculations. The child missing from the mill two months ago—the accepted theory was that it had tumbled into the millrace and been swept away; but the mother had always declared she had heard a shriek on the hill side of the house, in the opposite direction from the water. It was unthinkable, of course, but he wished that the boy had not made that uncanny remark about child flesh eaten two months ago. Such dreadful things should not be said even in fun.

Van Cheele, contrary to his usual wont, did not feel disposed to be communicative about his discovery in the wood. His position as a parish councillor and justice of the peace seemed somehow compromised by the fact that he was harbouring a personality of such doubtful repute on his property; there was even a possibility that a heavy bill of damages for raided lambs and poultry might be laid at his door. At dinner that night he was quite unusually silent.

"Where's your voice gone to?" said his aunt. "One would think you had seen a wolf."

Van Cheele, who was not familiar with the old saying, thought the remark rather foolish; if he *had* seen a wolf on his property his tongue would have been extraordinarily busy with the subject.

At breakfast next morning Van Cheele was conscious that his feeling of uneasiness regarding yesterday's episode had not wholly disappeared, and he resolved to go by train to the neighbouring cathedral town, hunt up Cunningham, and learn from him what he had really seen that had prompted the remark

about a wild beast in the woods. With this resolu-
tion taken, his usual cheerfulness partially returned,
and he hummed a bright little melody as he sauntered to the morning room for his customary cigarette. As he entered the room the melody made way
abruptly for a pious invocation. Gracefully asprawl
on the ottoman, in an attitude of almost exaggerated
repose, was the boy of the woods. He was drier than
when Van Cheele had last seen him, but no other al-
teration was noticeable in his toilet.

"How dare you come here?" asked Van Cheele fu-
riously.

"You told me I was not to stay in the woods," said
the boy calmly.

"But not to come here. Supposing my aunt should
see you!"

And with a view to minimizing that catastrophe
Van Cheele hastily obscured as much of his unwel-
come guest as possible under the folds of a *Morning
Post*. At that moment his aunt entered the room.

"This is a poor boy who has lost his way—and lost
his memory. He doesn't know who he is or where he
comes from," explained Van Cheele desperately,
glancing apprehensively at the waif's face to see
whether he was going to add inconvenient candour to
his other savage propensities.

Miss Van Cheele was enormously interested.

"Perhaps his underlinen is marked," she suggested.

"He seems to have lost most of that, too," said Van
Cheele, making frantic little grabs at the *Morning
Post* to keep it in its place.

A naked, homeless child appealed to Miss Van
Cheele as warmly as a stray kitten or derelict puppy
would have done.

"We must do all we can for him," she decided, and in a very short time a messenger, dispatched to the rectory, where a page boy was kept, had returned with a suit of pantry clothes, and the necessary accessories of shirt, shoes, collar, etc. Clothed, clean, and groomed, the boy lost none of his uncanniness in Van Cheele's eyes, but his aunt found him sweet.

"We must call him something till we know who he really is," she said. "Gabriel-Ernest, I think; those are nice suitable names."

Van Cheele agreed, but he privately doubted whether they were being grafted onto a nice suitable child. His misgivings were not diminished by the fact that his staid and elderly spaniel had bolted out of the house at the first incoming of the boy, and now obstinately remained shivering and yapping at the farther end of the orchard, while the canary, usually as vocally industrious as Van Cheele himself, had put itself on an allowance of frightened cheeps. More than ever he was resolved to consult Cunningham without loss of time.

As he drove off to the station his aunt was arranging that Gabriel-Ernest should help her to entertain the infant members of her Sunday-school class at tea that afternoon.

Cunningham was not at first disposed to be communicative.

"My mother died of some brain trouble," he explained, "so you will understand why I am averse to dwelling on anything of an impossibly fantastic nature that I may see or think that I have seen."

"But what *did* you see?" persisted Van Cheele.

"What I thought I saw was something so extraordinary that no really sane man could dignify it with the credit of having actually happened. I was standing, the last evening I was with you, half-hidden in the hedge growth by the orchard gate, watching the dying glow of the sunset. Suddenly I became aware of a naked boy, a bather from some neighbouring pool, I took him to be, who was standing out on the bare hillside also watching the sunset. His pose was so suggestive of some wild faun of Pagan myth that I instantly wanted to engage him as a model, and in another moment I think I should have hailed him. But just then the sun dipped out of view, and all the orange and pink slid out of the landscape, leaving it cold and grey. And at the same moment an astounding thing happened—the boy vanished too!"

"What! Vanished away into nothing?"

"No; that is the dreadful part of it," answered the artist; "on the open hillside where the boy had been standing a second ago, stood a large wolf, blackish in colour, with gleaming fangs and cruel, yellow eyes. You may think——"

But Van Cheele did not stop for anything as futile as thought. Already he was tearing at top speed towards the station. He dismissed the idea of a telegram. "Gabriel-Ernest is a werewolf" was a hopelessly inadequate effort at conveying the situation, and his aunt would think it was a code message to which he had omitted to give her the key. His one hope was that he might reach home before sundown. The cab which he chartered at the other end of the railway journey bore him with what seemed exasperating slowness along the country roads, which were pink and mauve with the flush of the sinking sun. His aunt was putting away some unfinished jams and cake when he arrived.

"Where is Gabriel-Ernest?" he almost screamed.

"He is taking the little Toop child home," said his aunt. "It was getting so late, I thought it wasn't safe to let it go back alone. What a lovely sunset, isn't it?"

But Van Cheele, although not oblivious of the glow in the western sky, did not stay to discuss its beauties. At a speed for which he was scarcely geared he raced along the narrow lane that led to the home of the Toops. On one side ran the swift current of the millstream, on the other rose the stretch of bare hillside. A dwindling rim of red sun showed still on the skyline, and the next turning must bring him in view of the ill-assorted couple he was pursuing. Then the colour went suddenly out of things, and a grey light settled itself with a quick shiver over the landscape. Van Cheele heard a shrill wail of fear, and stopped running.

Nothing was ever seen again of the Toops child or Gabriel-Ernest, but the latter's discarded garments were found lying in the road, so it was assumed that the child had fallen into the water, and that the boy had stripped and jumped in, in a vain endeavour to save it. Van Cheele and some workmen who were near by at the time testified to having heard a child scream loudly just near the spot where the clothes were found. Mrs. Toop, who had eleven other children, was decently resigned to her bereavement, but Miss Van Cheele sincerely mourned her lost foundling. It was on her initiative that a memorial brass was put up in the parish church to "Gabriel-Ernest, an unknown boy, who bravely sacrificed his life for another."

Van Cheele gave way to his aunt in most things, but he flatly refused to subscribe to the Gabriel-Ernest memorial.

The Bag

"THE MAJOR is coming in to tea," said Mrs. Hoopington to her niece. "He's just gone round to the stables with his horse. Be as bright and lively as you can; the poor man's got a fit of the glooms."

Major Pallaby was a victim of circumstances, over which he had no control, and of his temper, over which he had very little. He had taken on the Mastership of the Pexdale Hounds in succession to a highly popular man who had fallen foul of his committee, and the Major found himself confronted with the overt hostility of at least half the hunt, while his lack of tact and amiability had done much to alienate the remainder. Hence subscriptions were beginning to fall off, foxes grew provokingly scarcer, and wire obtruded itself with increasing frequency. The Major could plead reasonable excuse for his fit of the glooms.

In ranging herself as a partisan on the side of Major Pallaby, Mrs. Hoopington had been largely influenced by the fact that she had made up her mind to marry him at an early date. Against his notorious bad temper she set his three thousand a year, and his prospective succession to a baronetcy gave a casting vote in his favour. The Major's plans on the subject of matrimony were not at present in such an advanced stage as Mrs. Hoopington's, but he was begin-

ning to find his way over to Hoopington Hall with a
frequency that was already being commented on.

"He had a wretchedly thin field out again yesterday," said Mrs. Hoopington. "Why you didn't bring
one or two hunting men down with you, instead of
that stupid Russian boy, I can't think."

"Vladimir isn't stupid," protested her niece; "he's
one of the most amusing boys I ever met. Just com-
pare him for a moment with some of your heavy hunting me——"

"Anyhow, my dear Norah, he can't ride."

"Russians never can; but he shoots."

"Yes; and what does he shoot? Yesterday he brought
home a woodpecker in his gamebag."

"But he'd shot three pheasants and some rabbits as
well."

"That's no excuse for including a woodpecker in
his gamebag."

"Foreigners go in for mixed bags more than we do.
A grand duke pots a vulture just as seriously as we
should stalk a bustard. Anyhow, I've explained to
Vladimir that certain birds are beneath his dignity as
a sportsman. And as he's only nineteen, of course, his
dignity is a sure thing to appeal to."

Mrs. Hoopington sniffed. Most people with whom
Vladimir came in contact found his high spirits in-
fectious, but his present hostess was guaranteed im-
mune against infection of that sort.

"I hear him coming in now," she observed. "I
shall go and get ready for tea. We're going to have it
here in the hall. Entertain the Major if he comes in before I'm down, and, above all, be bright."

Norah was dependent on her aunt's good graces for
many little things that made life worth living, and she

was conscious of a feeling of discomfiture because
the Russian youth whom she had brought down as a
welcome element of change in the country-house rou-
tine was not making a good impression. That young
gentleman, however, was supremely unconscious of
any shortcomings, and burst into the hall, tired and
less sprucely groomed than usual, but distinctly ra-
diant. His gamebag looked comfortably full.

"Guess what I have shot," he demanded.

"Pheasants, wood pigeons, rabbits," hazarded
Norah.

"No; a large beast; I don't know what you call it in
English. Brown, with a darkish tail." Norah changed
colour.

"Does it live in a tree and eat nuts?" she asked,
hoping that the use of the adjective "large" might be
an exaggeration.

Vladimir laughed.

"Oh, no; not a *biyelka*."

"Does it swim and eat fish?" asked Norah, with a
fervent prayer in her heart that it might turn out to
be an otter.

"No," said Vladimir, busy with the straps of his
gamebag; "it lives in the woods, and eats rabbits and
chickens."

Norah sat down suddenly and hid her face in her
hands.

"Merciful Heaven!" she wailed; "he's shot a fox!"

Vladimir looked up at her in consternation. In a
torrent of agitated words she tried to explain the horror of the situation. The boy understood nothing, but
was thoroughly alarmed.

"Hide it, hide it!" said Norah frantically, pointing to
the still unopened bag. "My aunt and the Major will

be here in a moment. Throw it on the top of that chest; they won't see it there."

Vladimir swung the bag with fair aim; but the strap caught in its flight on the outstanding point of an antler fixed in the wall, and the bag, with its terrible burden, remained suspended just above the alcove where tea would presently be laid. At that moment Mrs. Hoopington and the Major entered the hall.

"The Major is going to draw our covers tomorrow," announced the lady, with a certain heavy satisfaction. "Smithers is confident that we'll be able to show him some sport; he swears he's seen a fox in the nut copse three times this week."

"I'm sure I hope so; I hope so," said the Major moodily. "I must break this sequence of blank days. One hears so often that a fox has settled down as a tenant for life in certain covers, and then when you go to turn him out there isn't a trace of him. I'm certain a fox was shot or trapped in Lady Widden's woods the very day before we drew them."

"Major, if anyone tried that game on in my woods they'd get short shrift," said Mrs. Hoopington.

Norah found her way mechanically to the tea table and made her fingers frantically busy in rearranging the parsley round the sandwich dish. On one side of her loomed the morose countenance of the Major, on the other she was conscious of the scared, miserable eyes of Vladimir. And above it all hung *that*. She dared not raise her eyes above the level of the tea table, and she almost expected to see a spot of accusing vulpine blood drip down and stain the whiteness of the cloth. Her aunt's manner signalled to her the repeated message to "be bright"; for the present she was fully occupied in keeping her teeth from chattering.

"What did you shoot today?" asked Mrs. Hoopington suddenly of the unusually silent Vladimir.

"Nothing—nothing worth speaking of," said the boy.

Norah's heart, which had stood still for a space, made up for lost time with a most disturbing bound.

"I wish you'd find something that was worth speaking about," said the hostess; "everyone seems to have lost their tongues."

"When did Smithers last see that fox?" said the Major.

"Yesterday morning; a fine dog fox, with a dark brush," confided Mrs. Hoopington.

"Aha, we'll have a good gallop after that brush tomorrow," said the Major, with a transient gleam of good humour. And then gloomy silence settled again round the tea table, a silence broken only by despondent munchings and the occasional feverish rattle of a teaspoon in its saucer. A diversion was at last afforded by Mrs. Hoopington's fox terrier, which had jumped onto a vacant chair, the better to survey the delicacies of the table, and was now sniffing in an upward direction at something apparently more interesting than cold teacake.

"What is exciting him?" asked his mistress, as the dog suddenly broke into short, angry barks, with a running accompaniment of tremulous whines.

"Why," she continued, "it's your gamebag, Vladimir! What have you got in it?"

"By Gad," said the Major, who was now standing up; "there's a pretty warm scent!"

And then a simultaneous idea flashed on himself and Mrs. Hoopington. Their faces flushed to distinct but harmonious tones of purple, and with one accusing voice they screamed, "You've shot the fox!"

Norah tried hastily to palliate Vladimir's misdeed in their eyes, but it is doubtful whether they heard her. The Major's fury clothed and reclothed itself in words as frantically as a woman up in town for one day's shopping tries on a succession of garments. He reviled and railed at fate and the general scheme of things; he pitied himself with a strong, deep pity too poignant for tears; he condemned everyone with whom he had ever come in contact to endless and abnormal punishments. In fact, he conveyed the impression that if a destroying angel had been lent to him for a week it would have had very little time for private study. In the lulls of his outcry could be heard the querulous monotone of Mrs. Hoopington and the sharp staccato barking of the fox terrier. Vladimir, who did not understand a tithe of what was being said, sat fondling a cigarette and repeating under his breath from time to time a vigorous English adjective which he had long ago taken affectionately into his vocabulary. His mind strayed back to the youth in the old Russian folktale who shot an enchanted bird with dramatic results. Meanwhile, the Major, roaming round the hall like an imprisoned cyclone, had caught sight of and joyfully pounced on the telephone apparatus, and lost no time in ringing up the hunt secretary and announcing his resignation of the Mastership. A servant had by this time brought his horse round to the door, and in a few seconds Mrs. Hoopington's shrill monotone had the field to itself. But after the Major's display her best efforts at vocal violence missed their full effect; it was as though one had come straight out from a Wagner opera into a rather tame thunderstorm. Realizing, perhaps, that her tirades were something of an anticlimax, Mrs. Hoopington broke suddenly into some rather necessary tears and marched out of the room, leaving behind her a silence almost as terrible as the turmoil which had preceded it.

"What shall I do with—*that*?" asked Vladimir at last.

"Bury it," said Norah.

"Just plain burial?" said Vladimir, rather relieved. He had almost expected that some of the local clergy would have insisted on being present, or that a salute might have to be fired over the grave.

And thus it came to pass that in the dusk of a November evening the Russian boy, murmuring a few of the prayers of his church for luck, gave hasty but decent burial to a large polecat under the lilac trees at Hoopington.

Tobermory

IT WAS a chill, rain-washed afternoon of a late August day, that indefinite season when partridges are still in security or cold storage, and there is nothing to hunt—unless one is bounded on the north by the Bristol Channel, in which case one may lawfully gallop after fat red stags. Lady Blemley's house party was not bounded on the north by the Bristol Channel, hence there was a full gathering of her guests round the tea table on this particular afternoon. And, in spite of the blankness of the season and the triteness of the occasion, there was no trace in the company of that fatigued restlessness which means a dread of the Pianola and a subdued hankering for auction bridge. The undisguised openmouthed attention of the entire party was fixed on the homely negative personality of Mr. Cornelius Appin. Of all her guests, he was the one who had come to Lady Blemley with the vaguest reputation. Someone had said he was "clever," and he had got his invitation in the moderate expectation, on the part of his hostess, that some portion at least of his cleverness would be contributed to the general entertainment. Until teatime that day she had been unable to discover in what direction, if any, his cleverness lay. He was neither a wit nor a croquet champion, a hypnotic

17

force nor a begetter of amateur theatricals. Neither
did his exterior suggest the sort of man in whom
women are willing to pardon a generous measure of
mental deficiency. He had subsided into mere Mr.
Appin, and the Cornelius seemed a piece of transparent baptismal bluff. And now he was claiming to
have launched on the world a discovery beside which
the invention of gunpowder, of the printing press,
and of steam locomotion were inconsiderable trifles.
Science had made bewildering strides in many direc-
tions during recent decades, but this thing seemed
to belong to the domain of miracle rather than to
scientific achievement.

"And do you really ask us to believe," Sir Wilfrid was
saying, "that you have discovered a means for in-
structing animals in the art of human speech, and
that dear old Tobermory has proved your first successful pupil?"

"It is a problem at which I have worked for the
last seventeen years," said Mr. Appin, "but only during
the last eight or nine months have I been rewarded
with glimmerings of success. Of course I have experi-
mented with thousands of animals, but latterly only
with cats, those wonderful creatures which have as-
similated themselves so marvellously with our civili-
zation while retaining all their highly developed
feral instincts. Here and there among cats one comes
across an outstanding superior intellect, just as one
does among the ruck of human beings, and when I
made the acquaintance of Tobermory a week ago I
saw at once that I was in contact with a 'Beyond-
cat' of extraordinary intelligence. I had gone far along
the road to success in recent experiments; with Tobermory, as you call him, I have reached the goal."

Mr. Appin concluded his remarkable statement in a voice which he strove to divest of a triumphant inflection. No one said "Rats," though Clovis' lips moved in a monosyllabic contortion, which probably invoked those rodents of disbelief.

"And do you mean to say," asked Miss Resker, after a slight pause, "that you have taught Tobermory to say and understand easy sentences of one syllable?"

"My dear Miss Resker," said the wonder-worker patiently, "one teaches little children and savages and backward adults in that piecemeal fashion; when one has once solved the problem of making a beginning with an animal of highly developed intelligence one has no need for those halting methods. Tobermory can speak our language with perfect correctness."

This time Clovis very distinctly said, "Beyond-rats!" Sir Wilfrid was more polite, but equally sceptical.

"Hadn't we better have the cat in and judge for ourselves?" suggested Lady Blemley.

Sir Wilfrid went in search of the animal, and the company settled themselves down to the languid expectation of witnessing some more or less adroit drawing-room ventriloquism.

In a minute Sir Wilfrid was back in the room, his face white beneath its tan and his eyes dilated with excitement.

"By Gad, it's true!"

His agitation was unmistakably genuine, and his hearers started forward in a thrill of awakened interest.

Collapsing into an armchair he continued breathlessly: "I found him dozing in the smoking room, and called out to him to come for his tea. He blinked at me in his usual way, and I said, 'Come on, Toby;

don't keep us waiting'; and, by Gad! he drawled out in a most horribly natural voice that he'd come when he dashed well pleased! I nearly jumped out of my skin!"

Appin had preached to absolutely incredulous hearers; Sir Wilfrid's statement carried instant conviction. A babel-like chorus of startled exclamation arose, amid which the scientist sat mutely enjoying the first fruit of his stupendous discovery.

In the midst of the clamour Tobermory entered the room and made his way with velvet tread and studied unconcern across to the group seated round the tea table.

A sudden hush of awkwardness and constraint fell on the company. Somehow there seemed an element of embarrassment in addressing on equal terms a domestic cat of acknowledged mental ability.

"Will you have some milk, Tobermory?" asked Lady Blemley in a rather strained voice.

"I don't mind if I do," was the response, couched in a tone of even indifference. A shiver of suppressed excitement went through the listeners, and Lady Blemley might be excused for pouring out the saucerful of milk rather unsteadily.

"I'm afraid I've split a good deal of it," she said.

"After all, it's not my Axminster," was Tobermory's rejoinder.

Another silence fell on the group, and then Miss Resker, in her best district-visitor manner, asked if the human language had been difficult to learn. Tobermory looked squarely at her for a moment and then fixed his gaze serenely on the middle distance. It was obvious that boring questions lay outside his scheme of life.

"What do you think of human intelligence?" asked Mavis Pellington lamely.

"Of whose intelligence in particular?" asked Tobermory coldly.

"Oh, well, mine for instance," said Mavis, with a feeble laugh.

"You put me in an embarrassing position," said Tobermory, whose tone and attitude certainly did not suggest a shred of embarrassment. "When your inclusion in this house party was suggested Sir Wilfrid protested that you were the most brainless woman of his acquaintance, and that there was a wide distinction between hospitality and the care of the feebleminded. Lady Blemley replied that your lack of brainpower was the precise quality which had earned you your invitation, as you were the only person she could think of who might be idiotic enough to buy their old car. You know, the one they call 'The Envy of Sisyphus,' because it goes quite nicely uphill if you push it."

Lady Blemley's protestations would have had greater effect if she had not casually suggested to Mavis only that morning that the car in question would be just the thing for her down at her Devonshire home.

Major Barfield plunged in heavily to effect a diversion.

"How about your carryings-on with the tortoiseshell puss up at the stables, eh?"

The moment he had said it everyone realized the blunder.

"One does not usually discuss these matters in public," said Tobermory frigidly. "From a slight observation of your ways since you've been in this

house I should imagine you'd find it inconvenient if I
were to shift the conversation onto your own little
affairs."

The panic which ensued was not confined to the
Major.

"Would you like to go and see if cook has got your
dinner ready?" suggested Lady Blemley hurriedly,
affecting to ignore the fact that it wanted at least
two hours to Tobermory's dinnertime.

"Thanks," said Tobermory, "Not quite so soon after
my tea. I don't want to die of indigestion."

"Cats have nine lives, you know," said Sir Wilfrid
heartily.

"Possibly," answered Tobermory; "but only one
liver."

"Adelaide!" said Mrs. Cornett, "do you mean to encourage that cat to go out and gossip about us in the
servants' hall?"

The panic had indeed become general. A narrow
ornamental balustrade ran in front of most of the
bedroom windows at the Towers, and it was recalled with dismay that this had formed a favourite
promenade for Tobermory at all hours, whence he
could watch the pigeons—and heaven knew what
else besides. If he intended to become reminiscent
in his present outspoken strain, the effect would be
something more than disconcerting. Mrs. Cornett, who
spent much time at her toilet table, and whose complexion was reputed to be of a nomadic though punc-
tual disposition, looked as ill at ease as the Major.
Miss Scrawen, who wrote fiercely sensuous poetry
and led a blameless life, merely displayed irritation;
if you are methodical and virtuous in private you
don't necessarily want everyone to know it. Bertie

van Tahn, who was so depraved at seventeen that he had long ago given up trying to be any worse, turned a dull shade of gardenia white, but he did not commit the error of dashing out of the room like Odo Finsberry, a young gentleman who was understood to be reading for the Church and who was possibly disturbed at the thought of scandals he might hear concerning other people. Clovis had the presence of mind to maintain a composed exterior; privately he was calculating how long it would take to procure a box of fancy mice through the agency of the *Exchange and Mart* as a species of hush money.

Even in a delicate situation like the present, Agnes Resker could not endure to remain too long in the background.

"Why did I ever come down here?" she asked dramatically.

Tobermory immediately accepted the opening.

"Judging by what you said to Mrs. Cornett on the croquet lawn yesterday, you were out for food. You described the Blemleys as the dullest people to stay with that you knew, but said they were clever enough to employ a first-rate cook; otherwise they'd find it difficult to get anyone to come down a second time."

"There's not a word of truth in it! I appeal to Mrs. Cornett——" exclaimed the discomfited Agnes.

"Mrs. Cornett repeated your remark afterwards to Bertie van Tahn," continued Tobermory, "and said, 'That woman is a regular Hunger Marcher; she'd go anywhere for four square meals a day,' and Bertie van Tahn said——"

At this point the chronicle mercifully ceased. Tobermory had caught a glimpse of the big yellow Tom from the rectory working his way through the shrubbery towards the stable wing. In a flash he had vanished through the open French window.

With the disappearance of his too brilliant pupil, Cornelius Appin found himself beset by a hurricane of bitter upbraiding, anxious inquiry, and frighter ed entreaty. The responsibility for the situation lay with him, and he must prevent matters from becoming worse. Could Tobermory impart his dangerous gift to other cats? was the first question he had to answer. It was possible, he replied, that he might have initiated his intimate friend the stable puss into his new accomplishment, but it was unlikely that his teaching could have taken a wider range as yet.

"Then," said Mrs. Cornett, "Tobermory may be a valuable cat and a great pet; but I'm sure you'll agree, Adelaide, that both he and the stable cat must be done away with without delay."

"You don't suppose I've enjoyed the last quarter of an hour, do you?" said Lady Blemley bitterly. "My husband and I are very fond of Tobermory—at least, we were before this horrible accomplishment was infused into him; but now, of course, the only thing is to have him destroyed as soon as possible."

"We can put some strychnine in the scraps he always gets at dinnertime," said Sir Wilfrid, "and I will go and drown the stable cat myself. The coachman will be very sore at losing his pet, but I'll say a very catching form of mange has broken out in both cats and we're afraid of it spreading to the kennels."

"But my great discovery!" expostulated Mr. Appin; "after all my years of research and experiment——"

"You can go and experiment on the shorthorns at the farm, who are under proper control," said Mrs.

Cornett, "or the elephants at the Zoological Gardens. They're said to be highly intelligent, and they have this recommendation, that they don't come creeping about our bedrooms and under chairs, and so forth."

An archangel ecstatically proclaiming the Millennium, and then finding that it clashed unpardonably with Henley and would have to be indefinitely postponed, could hardly have felt more crestfallen than Cornelius Appin at the reception of his wonderful achievement. Public opinion, however, was against him—in fact, had the general voice been consulted on the subject it is probable that a strong minority vote would have been in favour of including him in the strychnine diet.

Defective train arrangements and a nervous desire to see matters brought to a finish prevented an immediate dispersal of the party, but dinner that evening was not a social success. Sir Wilfrid had had rather a trying time with the stable cat and subsequently with the coachman. Agnes Resker ostentatiously limited her repast to a morsel of dry toast, which she bit as though it were a personal enemy; while Mavis Pellington maintained a vindictive silence throughout the meal. Lady Blemley kept up a flow of what she hoped was conversation, but her attention was fixed on the doorway. A plateful of carefully dosed fish scraps was in readiness on the sideboard, but sweets and savoury and dessert went their way, and no Tobermory appeared either in the dining room or kitchen.

The sepulchral dinner was cheerful compared with the subsequent vigil in the smoking room. Eating and drinking had at least supplied a distraction and cloak to the prevailing embarrassment. Bridge was out of the question in the general tension of nerves and tempers, and after Odo Finsberry had given a lugubrious rendering of "Mélisande in the Wood" to a frigid audience, music was tacitly avoided. At eleven the servants went to bed, announcing that the small window in the pantry had been left open as usual for Tobermory's private use. The guests read steadily through the current batch of magazines, and fell back gradually on the "Badminton Library" and bound volumes of *Punch*. Lady Blemley made periodic visits to the pantry, returning each time with an expression of listless depression which forestalled questioning.

At two o'clock Clovis broke the dominating silence.

"He won't turn up tonight. He's probably in the local newspaper office at the present moment, dictating the first instalment of his reminiscences. Lady What's-her-name's book won't be in it. It will be the event of the day."

Having made this contribution to the general cheerfulness, Clovis went to bed. At long intervals the various members of the house party followed his example.

The servants taking round the early tea made a uniform announcement in reply to a uniform question. Tobermory had not returned.

Breakfast was, if anything, a more unpleasant function than dinner had been, but before its conclusion the situation was relieved. Tobermory's corpse was brought in from the shrubbery, where a gardener had just discovered it. From the bites on his throat and the yellow fur which coated his claws it was evident that he had fallen in unequal combat with the big Tom from the rectory.

By midday most of the guests had quitted the Towers, and after lunch Lady Blemley had sufficiently recovered her spirits to write an extremely nasty letter to the rectory about the loss of her valuable pet.

Tobermory had been Appin's one successful pupil, and he was destined to have no successor. A few weeks later an elephant in the Dresden Zoological Garden, which had shown no previous signs of irritability, broke loose and killed an Englishman who had apparently been teasing it. The victim's name was variously reported in the papers as Oppin and Eppelin, but his front name was faithfully rendered Cornelius.

"If he was trying German irregular verbs on the poor beast," said Clovis, "he deserved all he got."

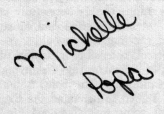

Mrs. Packletide's Tiger

IT WAS Mrs. Packletide's pleasure and intention that she should shoot a tiger. Not that the lust to kill had suddenly descended on her, or that she felt that she would leave India safer and more wholesome than she had found it, with one fraction less of wild beast per million of inhabitants. The compelling motive for her sudden deviation towards the footsteps of Nimrod was the fact that Loona Bimberton had recently been carried eleven miles in an aeroplane by an Algerian aviator, and talked of nothing else; only a personally procured tigerskin and a heavy harvest of press photographs could successfully counter that sort of thing. Mrs. Packletide had already arranged in her mind the lunch she would give at her house in Curzon Street, ostensibly in Loona Bimberton's honour, with a tigerskin rug occupying most of the foreground and all of the conversation. She had also already designed in her mind the tiger-claw brooch that she was going to give Loona Bimberton on her next birthday. In a world that is supposed to be chiefly swayed by hunger and by love Mrs. Packletide was an exception; her movements and motives were largely governed by dislike of Loona Bimberton.

Circumstances proved propitious. Mrs. Packletide

had offered a thousand rupees for the opportunity
of shooting a tiger without overmuch risk or exer-
tion, and it so happened that a neighbourhood village could boast of being the favoured rendezvous
of an animal of respectable antecedents, which had
been driven by the increasing infirmities of age to
abandon game-killing and confine its appetite to the
smaller domestic animals. The prospect of earning the
thousand rupees had stimulated the sporting and
commercial instinct of the villagers; children were
posted night and day on the outskirts of the local
jungle to head the tiger back in the unlikely event
of his attempting to roam away to fresh hunting
grounds, and the cheaper kinds of goats were left
about with elaborate carelessness to keep him satis-
fied with his present quarters. The one great anxiety
was lest he should die of old age before the date
appointed for the memsahib's shoot. Mothers carrying their babies home through the jungle after the
day's work in the fields hushed their singing lest they
might curtail the restful sleep of the venerable herd
robber.

The great night duly arrived, moonlit and cloudless.
A platform had been constructed in a comfortable
and conveniently placed tree, and thereon crouched
Mrs. Packletide and her paid companion, Miss Mebbin. A goat, gifted with a particularly persistent
bleat, such as even a partially deaf tiger might be
reasonably expected to hear on a still night, was
tethered at the correct distance. With an accurately
sighted rifle and a thumbnail pack of patience cards
the sportswoman awaited the coming of the quarry.

"I suppose we are in some danger?" said Miss
Mebbin.

She was not actually nervous about the wild beast, but she had a morbid dread of performing an atom more service than she had been paid for.

"Nonsense," said Mrs. Packletide; "it's a very old tiger. It couldn't spring up here even if it wanted to."

"If it's an old tiger I think you ought to get it cheaper. A thousand rupees is a lot of money."

Louisa Mebbin adopted a protective elder-sister attitude towards money in general, irrespective of nationality or denomination. Her energetic intervention had saved many a rouble from dissipating itself in tips in some Moscow hotel, and francs and centimes clung to her instinctively under circumstances which would have driven them headlong from less sympathetic hands. Her speculations as to the market depreciation of tiger remnants were cut short by the appearance on the scene of the animal itself. As soon as it caught sight of the tethered goat it lay flat on the earth, seemingly less from a desire to take advantage of all available cover than for the purpose of snatching a short rest before commencing the grand attack.

"I believe it's ill," said Louisa Mebbin, loudly in Hindustani, for the benefit of the village headman, who was in ambush in a neighbouring tree.

"Hush!" said Mrs. Packletide, and at that moment the tiger commenced ambling towards his victim.

"Now, now!" urged Miss Mebbin with some excitement; "if he doesn't touch the goat we needn't pay for it." (The bait was an extra.)

The rifle flashed out with a loud report, and the great tawny beast sprang to one side and then rolled over in the stillness of death. In a moment a crowd of excited natives had swarmed onto the scene, and

their shouting speedily carried the glad news to the
village, where a thumping of tom-toms took up the
chorus of triumph. And their triumph and rejoicing
found a ready echo in the heart of Mrs. Packletide;
already that luncheon party in Curzon Street seemed
immeasurably nearer.

It was Louisa Mebbin who drew attention to the
fact that the goat was in death throes from a mortal
bullet wound, while no trace of the rifle's deadly
word could be found on the tiger. Evidently the
wrong animal had been hit, and the beast of prey
had succumed to heart failure, caused by the sudden report of the rifle, accelerated by senile decay.
Mrs. Packletide was pardonably annoyed at the discovery; but, at any rate, she was the possessor of
a dead tiger, and the villagers, anxious for their
thousand rupees, gladly connived at the fiction that
she had shot the beast. And Miss Mebbin was a paid
companion. Therefore did Mrs. Packletide face the
cameras with a light heart, and her pictured fame
reached from the pages of the *Texas Weekly Snap-
shot* to the illustrated Monday supplement of the
Novoe Vremya. As for Loona Bimberton, she refused
to look at an illustrated paper for weeks, and her
letter of thanks for the gift of a tiger-claw brooch
was a model of repressed emotions. The luncheon
party she declined; there are limits beyond which
repressed emotions become dangerous.

From Curzon Street the tigerskin rug traveled
down to the Manor House, and was duly inspected
and admired by the county, and it seemed a fitting
and appropriate thing when Mrs. Packletide went

to the County Costume Ball in the character of Diana. She refused to fall in, however, with Clovis' tempting suggestion of a primeval dance party, at which every one should wear the skins of beasts they had recently slain. "I should be in rather a Baby Bunting condition," confessed Clovis, "with a miserable rabbitskin or two to wrap up in, but then," he added, with a rather malicious glance at Diana's proportions, "my figure is quite as good as that Russian dancing boy's."

"How amused every one would be if they knew what really happened," said Louisa Mebbin a few days after the ball.

"What do you mean?" asked Mrs. Packletide quickly.

"How you shot the goat and frightened the tiger to death," said Miss Mebbin, with her disagreeably pleasant laugh.

"No one would believe it," said Mrs. Packletide, her face changing colour as rapidly as though it were going through a book of patterns before post time.

"Loona Bimberton would," said Miss Mebbin. Mrs. Packletide's face settled on an unbecoming shade of greenish white.

"You surely wouldn't give me away?" she asked.

"I've seen a weekend cottage near Dorking that I should rather like to buy," said Miss Mebbin with seeming irrelevance. "Six hundred and eighty, freehold. Quite a bargain, only I don't happen to have the money."

Louisa Mebbin's pretty weekend cottage, christened by her "Les Fauves," and gay in summertime with its garden borders of tiger lilies, is the wonder and admiration of her friends.

"It is a marvel how Louisa manages to do it," is the general verdict.

Mrs. Packletide indulges in no more big-game shooting.

"The incidental expenses are so heavy," she confides to inquiring friends.

Sredni Vashtar

CONRADIN was ten years old, and the doctor had pronounced his professional opinion that the boy would not live another five years. The doctor was silky and effete, and counted for little, but his opinion was endorsed by Mrs. De Ropp, who counted for nearly everything. Mrs. De Ropp was Conradin's cousin and guardian, and in his eyes she represented those three fifths of the world that are necessary and disagreeable and real; the other two-fifths, in perpetual antagonism to the foregoing, were summed up in himself and his imagination. One of these days Conradin supposed he would. succumb to the mastering pressure of wearisome necessary things—such as illnesses and coddling restrictions and drawn-out dullness. Without his imagination, which was rampant under the spur of loneliness, he would have succumbed long ago.

Mrs. De Ropp would never, in her honestest moments, have confessed to herself that she disliked Conradin, though she might have been dimly aware that thwarting him "for his good" was a duty which she did not find particularly irksome. Conradin hated her with a desperate sincerity which he was perfectly able to mask. Such few pleasures as he could contrive for himself gained an added relish from the likelihood that they would be displeasing to his guardian, and from the realm of his imagination she was locked out—an unclean thing, which should find no entrance.

In the dull, cheerless garden, overlooked by so many windows that were ready to open with a message not to do this or that, or a reminder that medicines were due, he found little attraction. The few fruit trees that it contained were set jealously apart from his plucking, as though they were rare specimens of their kind blooming in an arid waste; it would probably have been difficult to find a market gardener who would have offered ten shillings for their entire yearly produce. In a forgotten corner, however, almost hidden behind a dismal shrubbery, was a disused tool shed of respectable proportions, and within its walls Conradin found a haven, something that took on the varying aspects of a playroom and a cathedral. He had peopled it with a legion of familiar phantoms, evoked partly from fragments of history and partly from his own brain, but it also boasted two inmates of flesh and blood. In one corner lived a ragged-plumaged Houdan hen, on which the boy lavished an affection that had scarcely another outlet. Farther back in the gloom stood a large hutch, divided into two compartments, one of which was fronted with close iron bars. This was the abode of a large polecat-ferret, which a friendly butcher boy had once smuggled, cage and all, into its present quarters, in exchange for a long-secreted hoard of small silver. Conradin was dreadfully afraid of the lithe, sharpfanged beast, but it was his most treasured possession. Its very presence in the tool shed was a secret and fearful joy, to be kept scrupulously

from the knowledge of the Woman, as he privately
dubbed his cousin. And one day, out of Heaven
knows what material, he spun the beast a wonderful
name, and from that moment it grew into a god and
a religion. The Woman indulged in religion once
a week at a church near by, and took Conradin with
her, but to him the church service was an alien rite in
the House of Rimmon. Every Thursday, in the dim
and musty silence of the tool shed, he worshipped
with mystic and elaborate ceremonial before the
wooden hutch where dwelt Sredni Vashtar, the great
ferret. Red flowers in their season and scarlet ber-
ries in the wintertime were offered at his shrine, for
he was a god who laid some special stress on the
fierce impatient side of things, as opposed to the
Woman's religion, which, as far as Conradin could
observe, went to great lengths in the contrary direction. And on great festivals powered nutmeg was
strewn in front of his hutch, an important feature
of the offering being that the nutmeg had to be stolen.
These festivals were of irregular occurrence, and were
chiefly appointed to celebrate some passing event.
On one occasion, when Mrs. De Ropp suffered from
acute toothache for three days, Conradin kept up the
festival during the entire three days, and almost suc-
ceeded in persuading himself that Sredni Vashtar was
personally responsible for the toothache. If the malady had lasted for another day the supply of nutmeg would have given out.

The Houdan hen was never drawn into the cult
of Sredni Vashtar. Conradin had long ago settled that
she was an Anabaptist. He did not pretend to have
the remotest knowledge as to what an Anabaptist

was, but he privately hoped that it was dashing and not very respectable. Mrs. De Ropp was the ground plan on which he based and detested all respectability.

After a while Conradin's absorption in the tool shed began to attract the notice of his guardian. "It is not good for him to be pottering down there in all weathers," she promptly decided, and at breakfast one morning she announced that the Houdan hen had been sold and taken away overnight. With her shortsighted eyes she peered at Conradin, waiting for an outbreak of rage and sorrow, which she was ready to rebuke with a flow of excellent precepts and reasoning. But Conradin said nothing; there was nothing to be said. Something perhaps in his white set face gave her a momentary qualm, for at tea that afternoon there was toast on the table, a delicacy which she usually banned on the ground that it was bad for him; also because the making of it "gave trouble," a deadly offence in the middle-class feminine eye.

"I thought you liked toast," she exclaimed, with an injured air, observing that he did not touch it.

"Sometimes," said Conradin.

In the shed that evening there was an innovation in the worship of the hutch god. Conradin had been wont to chant his praises; tonight he asked a boon.

"Do one thing for me, Sredni Vashtar."

The thing was not specified. As Sredni Vashtar was a god he must be supposed to know. And choking back a sob as he looked at that other empty corner, Conradin went back to the world he so hated.

And every night, in the welcome darkness of his

bedroom, and every evening in the dusk of the tool shed, Conradin's bitter litany went up: "Do one thing for me, Sredni Vashtar."

Mrs. De Ropp noticed that the visits to the shed did not cease, and one day she made a further journey of inspection.

"What are you keeping in that locked hutch?" she asked. "I believe it's guinea pigs. I'll have them all cleared away."

Conradin shut his lips tight, but the Woman ransacked his bedroom till she found the carefully hidden key, and forthwith marched down to the shed to complete her discovery. It was a cold afternoon, and Conradin had been bidden to keep to the house. From the farthest window of the dining room the door of the shed could just be seen beyond the corner of the shrubbery, and there Conradin stationed himself. He saw the Woman enter, and then he imagined her opening the door of the sacred hutch and peering down with her shortsighted eyes into the thick straw bed where his god lay hidden. Perhaps she would prod at the straw in her clumsy impatience. And Conradin fervently breathed his prayer for the last time. But he knew as he prayed that he did not believe. He knew that the Woman would come out presently with that pursed smile he loathed so well on her face, and that in an hour or two the gardener would carry away his wonderful god, a god no longer, but a simple brown ferret in a hutch. And he knew that the Woman would triumph always as she triumphed now, and that he would grow ever more sickly under her pestering and domineering and superior wisdom, till one day nothing would matter much more with him, and the doctor would be proved right. And in

the sting and misery of his defeat, he began to chant
loudly and defiantly the hymn of his threatened idol:

> *Sredni Vashtar went forth,*
> *His thoughts were red thoughts and his teeth*
> *were white.*
> *His enemies called for peace, but he brought*
> *them death.*
> *Sredni Vashtar the Beautiful.*

And then of a sudden he stopped his chanting and
drew closer to the windowpane. The door of the shed
still stood ajar as it had been left, and the minutes
were slipping by. They were long minutes, but they
slipped by nevertheless. He watched the starlings
running and flying in little parties across the lawn;
he counted them over and over again, with one eye
always on that swinging door. A sour-faced maid
came in to lay the table for tea, and still Conradin
stood and waited and watched. Hope had crept by
inches into his heart, and now a look of triumph began to blaze in his eyes that he had only known the
wistful patience of defeat. Under his breath, with a
furtive exultation, he began once again the paean of
victory and devastation. And presently his eyes
were rewarded: out through that doorway came a
long, low, yellow-and-brown beast, with eyes a-blink
at the waning daylight, and dark wet stains around
the fur of jaws and throat. Conradin dropped on his
knees. The great polecat ferret made its way down
to a small brook at the foot of the garden, drank
for a moment, then crossed a little plank bridge
and was lost to sight in the bushes. Such was the
passing of Sredni Vashtar.

"Tea is ready," said the maid; "where is the mistress?"

"She went down to the shed some time ago," said Conradin.

And while the maid went to summon her mistress to tea, Conradin fished a toasting fork out of the sideboard drawer and proceeded to toast himself a piece of bread. And during the toasting of it and the buttering of it with much butter and the slow enjoyment of eating it, Conradin listened to the noises and silences which fell in quick spasms beyond the dining-room door. The loud, foolish screaming of the maid, the answering chorus of wondering ejaculations from the kitchen region, the scuttering footsteps and hurried embassies for outside help, and then, after a lull, the scared sobbings and the shuffling tread of those who bore a heavy burden into the house.

"Whoever will break it to the poor child? I couldn't for the life of me!" exclaimed a shrill voice. And while they debated the matter among themselves, Conradin made himself another piece of toast.

The Easter Egg

I**T WAS** distinctly hard lines for Lady Barbara, who came of good fighting stock, and was one of the bravest women of her generation, that her son should be so undisguisedly a coward. Whatever good qualities Lester Slaggby may have possessed, and he was in some respects charming, courage could certainly never be imputed to him. As a child he had suffered from childish timidity, as a boy from unboyish funk, and as a youth he had exchanged unreasoning fears for others which were more formidable from the fact of having a carefully-thought-out basis. He was frankly afraid of animals, nervous with firearms, and never crossed the Channel without mentally comparing the numerical proportion of life belts to passengers. On horseback he seemed to require as many hands as a Hindu god, at least four for clutching the reins, and two more for patting the horse soothingly on the neck. Lady Barbara no longer pretended not to see her son's prevailing weakness; with her usual courage she faced the knowledge of it squarely, and motherlike, loved him none the less.

Continental travel, anywhere away from the great tourist tracks, was a favoured hobby with Lady Barbara, and Lester joined her as often as possible.

Eastertide usually found her at Knobaltheim, an up-
land township in one of those small princedoms that
make inconspicuous freckles on the map of Central
Europe.

A long-standing acquaintanceship with the reign-
ing family made her a personage of due importance
in the eyes of her old friend the Burgomaster, and
she was anxiously consulted by that worthy on the
momentous occasion when the Prince made known
his intention of coming in person to open a sana-
torium outside the town. All the usual items in a programme of welcome, some of them fatuous and commonplace, others quaint and charming, had been arranged for, but the Burgomaster hoped that the re-
sourceful English lady might have something new
and tasteful to suggest in the way of loyal greeting.
The Prince was known to the outside world, if at all,
as an old-fashioned reactionary, combating modern
progress, as it were, with a wooden sword; to his
own people he was known as a kindly old gentleman with a certain endearing stateliness which had
nothing of standoffishness about it. Knobaltheim was
anxious to do its best. Lady Barbara discussed the
matter with Lester and one or two acquaintances in
her little hotel, but ideas were difficult to come by.

"Might I suggest something to the Gnädige Frau?"
asked a sallow, high-cheekboned lady to whom the
Englishwoman had spoken once or twice, and whom
she had set down in her mind as probably a Southern
Slav.

"Might I suggest something for the Reception
Feast?" she went on, with a certain shy eagerness.
"Our little child here, our baby, we will dress him
in little white coat, with small wings, as an Easter

angel, and he will carry a large white Easter egg, and inside shall be a basket of plover eggs, of which the Prince is so fond, and he shall give it to his Highness as Easter offering. It is so pretty an idea; we have seen it done once in Styria."

Lady Barbara looked dubiously at the proposed Easter angel, a fair, wooden-faced child of about four years old. She had noticed it the day before in the hotel, and wondered rather how such a tow-headed child could belong to such a dark-visaged couple as the woman and her husband; probably, she thought, an adopted baby, especially as the couple were not young.

"Of course, Gnädige Frau will escort the little child up to the Prince," pursued the woman; "but he will be quite good, and do as he is told."

"We haf some pluffers' eggs shall come fresh from Wien," said the husband.

The small child and Lady Barbara seemed equally unenthusiastic about the pretty idea; Lester was openly discouraging, but when the Burgomaster heard of it he was enchanted. The combination of sentiment and plovers' eggs appealed strongly to his Teutonic mind.

On the eventful day the Easter angel, really quite prettily and quaintly dressed, was a centre of kindly interest to the gala crowd marshalled to receive his Highness. The mother was unobtrusive and less fancy than most parents would have been under the circumstances, merely stipulating that she should place the Easter egg herself in the arms that had been carefully schooled how to hold the precious burden. Then Lady Barbara moved forward, the child marching stolidly and with grim determination at her

side. It had been promised cakes and sweeties galore
if it gave the egg well and truly to the kind old
gentleman who was waiting to receive it. Lester had
tried to convey to it privately that horrible smackings
would attend any failure in its share of the proceed-
ings, but it is doubtful if his German caused more
than an immediate distress. Lady Barbara had thoughtfully provided herself with an emergency supply of
chocolate sweetmeats; children may sometimes be
timeservers, but they do not encourage long accounts.
As they approached near to the princely dais Lady
Barbara stood discreetly aside, and the stolid-faced
infant walked forward alone, with staggering but
steadfast gait, encouraged by a murmur of elderly
approval. Lester, standing in the front row of the onlookers, turned to scan the crowd for the beaming
faces of the happy parents. In a side road which
led to the railway station he saw a cab; entering
the cab with every appearance of furtive haste were
the dark-visaged couple who had been so plausibly
eager for the "pretty idea." The sharpened instinct
of cowardice lit up the situation to him in one
swift flash. The blood roared and surged to his head
as though thousands of floodgates had been opened
in his veins and arteries, and his brain was the com-
mon sluice in which all the torrents met. He saw
nothing but a blur around him. Then the blood
ebbed away in quick waves, till his very heart
seemed drained and empty, and he stood nerve-
lessly, helplessly, dumbly watching the child, bearing its accursed burden with slow, relentless steps
nearer and nearer to the group that waited sheep-
like to receive him. A fascinated curiosity com-
pelled Lester to turn his head towards the fugitives;

the cab had started at hot pace in the direction of the station.

The next moment Lester was running, running faster than any of those present had ever seen a man run, and—he was not running away. For that stray fraction of his life some unwonted impulse beset him, some hint of the stock he came from, and he ran unflinchingly towards danger. He stooped and clutched at the Easter egg as one tries to scoop up the ball in Rugby football. What he meant to do with it he had not considered, the thing was to get it. But the child had been promised cakes and sweetmeats if it safely gave the egg into the hands of the kindly old gentleman; it uttered no scream, but it held to its charge with limpet grip. Lester sank to his knees, tugging savagely at the tightly clasped burden, and angry cries rose from the scandalized onlookers. A questioning, threatening ring formed round him, then shrank back in recoil as he shrieked out one hideous word. Lady Barbara heard the word and saw the crowd race away like scattered sheep, saw the Prince forcibly hustled away by his attendants; also she saw her son lying prone in an agony of overmastering terror, his spasm of daring shattered by the child's unexpected resistance, still clutching frantically, as though for safety, at that white-satin gewgaw, unable to crawl even from its deadly neighbourhood, able only to scream and scream and scream. In her brain she was dimly conscious of balancing, or striving to balance, the abject shame which had him now in thrall against the one compelling act of courage which had flung him grandly and madly on to the point of danger. It was only for the fraction of a minute that she stood watching the two entangled figures, the infant with its woodenly obstinate face and body tense with dogged resistance, and the boy limp and already nearly dead with a terror that almost stifled his screams; and over them the long gala streamers flapping gaily in the sunshine. She never forgot the scene; but then, it was the last she ever saw.

Lady Barbara carries her scarred face with its sightless eyes as bravely as ever in the world, but at Eastertide her friends are careful to keep from her ears any mention of the children's Easter symbol.

Filboid Studge,
the Story of
a Mouse That Helped

"**I** WANT to marry your daughter," said Mark Spayley with faltering eagerness. "I am only an artist with an income of two hundred a year, and she is the daughter of an enormously wealthy man, so I suppose you will think my offer a piece of presumption."

Duncan Dullamy, the great company inflator, showed no outward sign of displeasure. As a matter of fact, he was secretly relieved at the prospect of finding even a two-hundred-a-year husband for his daughter Leonore. A crisis was rapidly rushing upon him, from which he knew he would emerge with neither money nor credit; all his recent ventures had fallen flat, and flattest of all had gone the wonderful new breakfast food, Pipenta, on the advertisement of which he had sunk such huge sums. It could scarcely be called a drug in the market; people bought drugs, but no one bought Pipenta.

"Would you marry Leonore if she were a poor man's daughter?" asked the man of phantom wealth.

"Yes," said Mark, wisely avoiding the error of over protestation. And to his astonishment Leonore's father not only gave his consent, but suggested a fairly early date for the wedding.

"I wish I could show my gratitude in some way," said Mark with genuine emotion. "I'm afraid it's rather like the mouse proposing to help the lion."

"Get people to buy that beastly muck," said Dullamy, nodding savagely at a poster of the despised Pipenta, "and you'll have done more than any of my agents have been able to accomplish."

"It wants a better name," said Mark reflectively, "and something distinctive in the poster line. Anyway, I'll have a shot at it."

Three weeks later the world was advised of the coming of a new breakfast food, heralded under the resounding name of "Filboid Studge." Spayley put forth no pictures of massive babies springing up with funguslike rapidity under its forcing influence, or of representatives of the leading nations of the world scrambling with fatuous eagerness for its possession. One huge sombre poster depicted the Damned in Hell suffering a new torment from the inability to get the Filboid Studge which elegant young fiends held in transparent bowls just beyond their reach. The scene was rendered even more gruesome by a subtle suggestion of the features of leading men and women of the day in the portrayal of the Lost Souls; prominent individuals of both political parties, Society hostesses, well-known dramatic authors and novelists, and distinguished aeroplanists were dimly recognizable in that doomed throng; noted lights of the musical-comedy stage flickered wanly in the shades of the Inferno, smiling still from force of habit, but with the fearsome smiling rage of baffled effort. The poster bore no fulsome allusions to the merits of the new breakfast food; but a single grim statement ran in bold letters along its base: "They cannot buy it now."

Spayley had grasped the fact that people will do things from a sense of duty which they would never attempt as a pleasure. There are thousands of respectable middle-class men who, if you found them unexpectedly in a Turkish bath, would explain in all sincerity that the doctor had ordered them to take Turkish baths; if you told them in return that you went there because you like it, they would stare in pained wonder at the frivolity of your motive. In the same way, whenever a massacre of Armenians is reported from Asia Minor, every one assumes that it has been carried out "under orders" from somewhere or another; no one seems to think that there are people who might *like* to kill their neighbours now and then.

And so it was with the new breakfast food. No one would have eaten Filboid Studge as a pleasure, but the grim austerity of its advertisement drove housewives in shoals to the grocers' shops to clamour for an immediate supply. In small kitchens solemn pigtailed daughters helped depressed mothers to perform the primitive ritual of its preparation. On the breakfast tables of cheerless parlours it was partaken of in silence. Once the womenfolk discovered that it was thoroughly unpalatable, their zeal in forcing it on their households knew no bounds. "You haven't eaten your Filboid Studge!" would be screamed at the appetiteless clerk as he hurried wearily from the breakfast table, and his evening meal would be prefaced by a warmed-up mess which would be explained as "your Filboid Studge that you didn't eat this morning." Those strange fanatics who ostentatiously mortify themselves, inwardly and outwardly, with health biscuits and health garments, battened aggressively on the new food. Earnest spectacled young men devoured it on the steps of the National Liberal Club. A bishop who did not believe in a future state preached against the poster, and a peer's daughter died from eating too much of the compound. A further advertisement was obtained when an infantry regiment mutinied and shot its officers rather than eat the nauseous mess; fortunately, Lord Birrell of Blatherstone, who was War Minister at the moment, saved the situation by his happy epigram, that "Discipline to be effective must be optional."

Filboid Studge had become a household word, but Dullamy wisely realized that it was not necessarily the last word in breakfast dietary; its supremacy would be challenged as soon as some yet more unpalatable food should be put on the market. There might even be a reaction in favour of something tasty and appetizing, and the Puritan austerity of the moment might be banished from domestic cookery. At an opportune moment, therefore, he sold out his interests in the article which had brought him in colossal wealth at a critical juncture, and placed his financial reputation beyond the reach of cavil. As for Leonore, who was now an heiress on a far greater scale than ever before, he naturally found her something a vast deal higher in the husband market than a two-hundred-a-year poster designer. Mark Spayley, the brain mouse who had helped the financial lion with such untoward effect, was left to curse the day he produced the wonder-working poster.

"After all," said Clovis, meeting him shortly afterwards at his club, "you have this doubtful consolation, that 'tis not in mortals to countermand success."

Laura

"Y̶OU ARE not really dying, are you?" asked Amanda. "I have the doctor's permission to live till Tuesday," said Laura.

"But today is Saturday; this is serious!" gasped Amanda.

"I don't know about it being serious; it is certainly Saturday," said Laura.

"Death is always serious," said Amanda.

"I never said I was going to die. I am presumably going to leave off being Laura, but I shall go on being something. An animal of some kind, I suppose. You see, when one hasn't been very good in the life one has just lived, one reincarnates in some lower organism. And I haven't been very good, when one comes to think of it. I've been petty and mean and vindictive and all that sort of thing when circumstances have seemed to warrant it."

"Circumstances never warrant that sort of thing," said Amanda hastily.

"If you don't mind my saying so," observed Laura, "Egbert is a circumstance that would warrant any amount of that sort of thing. You're married to him —that's different; you've sworn to love, honour, and endure him: I haven't."

"I don't see what's wrong with Egbert," protested Amanda.

"Oh, I dare say the wrongness has been on my part," admitted Laura dispassionately; "he has merely been the extenuating circumstance. He made a thin, peevish kind of fuss, for instance, when I took the collie puppies from the farm out for a run the other day."

"They chased his young broods of speckled Sussex and drove two sitting hens off their nests, besides running all over the flower beds. You know how devoted he is to his poultry and garden."

"Anyhow, he needn't have gone on about it for the entire evening and then have said, 'Let's say no more about it' just when I was beginning to enjoy the discussion. That's where one of my petty, vindictive revenges came in," added Laura with an unrepentant chuckle; "I turned the entire family of speckled Sussex into his seedling shed the day after the puppy episode."

"How could you?" exclaimed Amanda.

"It came quite easy," said Laura; "two of the hens pretended to be laying at the time, but I was firm."

"And we thought it was an accident!"

"You see," resumed Laura, "I really *have* some grounds for supposing that my next incarnation will be in a lower organism. I shall be an animal of some kind. On the other hand, I haven't been a bad sort in my way, so I think I may count on being a nice animal, something elegant and lively, with a love of fun. An otter, perhaps."

"I can't imagine you as an otter," said Amanda.

"Well, I don't suppose you can imagine me as an angel, if it comes to that," said Laura.

Amanda was silent. She couldn't.

"Personally I think an otter life would be rather enjoyable," continued Laura; "salmon to eat all the year round, and the satisfaction of being able to fetch the trout in their own homes without having to wait for hours till they condescend to rise to the fly you've been dangling before them; and an elegant svelte figure——"

"Think of the otter hounds," interposed Amanda; "how dreadful to be hunted and harried and finally worried to death!"

"Rather fun with half the neighbourhood looking on, and anyhow not worse than this Saturday-to-Tuesday business of dying by inches; and then I should go on into something else. If I had been a moderately good otter I suppose I should get back into human shape of some sort; probably something rather primitive—a little brown, unclothed Nubian boy, I should think."

"I wish you would be serious," sighed Amanda; "you really ought to be if you're only going to live till Tuesday."

"So dreadfully upsetting," Amanda complained to her uncle-in-law, Sir Lulworth Quayne. "I've asked quite a lot of people down for golf and fishing, and the rhododendrons are just looking their best."

"Laura always was inconsiderate," said Sir Lulworth; "she was born during Goodwood week, with an ambassador staying in the house who hated babies."

"She had the maddest kind of ideas," said Amanda; "do you know if there was any insanity in her family?"

"Insanity? No, I never heard of any. Her father

lives in West Kensington, but I believe he's sane on all other subjects."

"She had an idea that she was going to be reincarnated as an otter," said Amanda.

"One meets with those ideas of reincarnation so frequently, even in the West," said Sir Lulworth, "that one can hardly set them down as being mad. And Laura was such an unaccountable person in this life that I should not like to lay down definite rules as to what she might be doing in an afterstate."

"You think she really might have passed into some animal form?" asked Amanda. She was one of those who shape their opinions rather readily from the standpoint of those around them.

Just then Egbert entered the breakfast room, wearing an air of bereavement that Laura's demise would have been insufficient, in itself, to account for.

"Four of my speckled Sussex have been killed," he exclaimed; "the very four that were to go to the show on Friday. One of them was dragged away and eaten right in the middle of the new carnation bed that I've been to such trouble and expense over. My best flower bed and my best fowls singled out for destruction; it almost seems as if the brute that did the deed had special knowledge how to be as devastating as possible in a short space of time."

"Was it a fox, do you think?" asked Amanda.

"Sounds more like a polecat," said Sir Lulworth.

"No," said Egbert, "there were marks of webbed feet all over the place, and we followed the tracks down to the stream at the bottom of the garden; evidently an otter."

Amanda looked quickly and furtively across at Sir Lulworth.

Egbert was too agitated to eat any breakfast, and went out to superintend the strengthening of the poultry yard defences.

"I think she might at least have waited till the funeral was over," said Amanda in a scandalized voice.

"It's her own funeral, you know," said Sir Lulworth; "it's a nice point in etiquette how far one ought to show respect to one's own mortal remains."

Disregard for mortuary convention was carried to further lengths next day; during the absence of the family at the funeral ceremony the remaining survivors of the speckled Sussex were massacred. The marauder's line of retreat seemed to have embraced most of the flower beds on the lawn, but the strawberry beds in the lower garden had also suffered.

"I shall get the otter hounds to come here at the earliest possible moment," said Egbert savagely.

"On no account! You can't dream of such a thing!" exclaimed Amanda. "I mean, it wouldn't do, so soon after a funeral in the house."

"It's a case of necessity," said Egbert; "Once an otter takes to that sort of thing it won't stop."

"Perhaps it will go elsewhere now that there are no more fowls left," suggested Amanda.

"One would think you wanted to shield the beast," said Egbert.

"There's been so little water in the stream lately," objected Amanda; "it seems hardly sporting to hunt an animal when it has so little chance of taking refuge anywhere."

"Good gracious!" fumed Egbert. "I'm not thinking about sport. I want to have the animal killed as soon as possible."

Even Amanda's opposition weakened when, during

church time on the following Sunday, the otter made
its way into the house, raided half a salmon from the
larder, and worried it into scaly fragments on the
Persian rug in Egbert's studio.

"We shall have it hiding under our beds and biting
pieces out of our feet before long," said Egbert, and
from what Amanda knew of this particular otter she
felt that the possibility was not a remote one.

On the evening preceding the day fixed for the hunt
Amanda spent a solitary hour walking by the banks of
the stream, making what she imagined to be hound
noises. It was charitably supposed by those who over-
heard her performance that she was practising for
farmyard imitations at the forthcoming village entertainment.

It was her friend and neighbour, Aurora Burret,
who brought her news of the day's sport.

"Pity you weren't out; we had quite a good day.
We found at once, in the pool just below your garden."

"Did you—kill?" asked Amanda.

"Rather. A fine she-otter. Your husband got rather
badly bitten in trying to 'tail it.' Poor beast, I felt
quite sorry for it, it had such a human look in its eyes
when it was killed. You'll call me silly, but do you
know who the look reminded me of? My dear woman,
what is the matter?"

When Amanda had recovered to a certain extent
from her attack of nervous prostration Egbert took
her to the Nile Valley to recuperate. Change of scene
speedily brought about the desired recovery of health
and mental balance. The escapades of an adventurous
otter in search of a variation of diet were viewed in
their proper light. Amanda's normally placid tempera-

ment reasserted itself. Even a hurricane of shouted curses, coming from her husband's dressing room, in her husband's voice, but hardly in his usual vocabulary, failed to disturb her serenity as she made a leisurely toilet one evening in a Cairo hotel.

"What is the matter? What has happened?" she asked in amused curiosity.

"The little beast has thrown all my clean shirts into the bath! Wait till I catch you, you little——"

"What little beast?" asked Amanda, suppressing a desire to laugh; Egbert's language was so hopelessly inadequate to express his outraged feelings.

"A little beast of a naked brown Nubian boy," spluttered Egbert.

And now Amanda is seriously ill.

The Open Window

"**M**Y AUNT will be down presently, Mr. Nuttel," said a very self-possessed young lady of fifteen; "in the meantime you must try and put up with me."

Framton Nuttel endeavoured to say the correct something which should duly flatter the niece of the moment without unduly discounting the aunt that was to come. Privately he doubted more than ever whether these formal visits on a succession of total strangers would do much towards helping the nerve cure which he was supposed to be undergoing.

"I know how it will be," his sister had said when he was preparing to migrate to this rural retreat; "you will bury yourself down there and not speak to a living soul, and your nerves will be worse than ever from moping. I shall just give you letters of introduction to all the people I know there. Some of them, as far as I can remember, were quite nice."

Framton wondered whether Mrs. Sappleton, the lady to whom he was presenting one of the letters of introduction, came into the nice division.

"Do you know many of the people round here?" asked the niece, when she judged that they had had sufficient silent communion.

"Hardly a soul," said Framton. "My sister was staying here, at the Rectory, you know, some four years ago, and she gave me letters of introduction to some of the people here."

He made the last statement in a tone of distinct regret.

"Then you know practically nothing about my aunt?" pursued the self-possessed young lady.

"Only her name and address," admitted the caller. He was wondering whether Mrs. Sappleton was in the married or widowed state. An undefinable something about the room seemed to suggest masculine habitation.

"Her great tragedy happened just three years ago," said the child; "that would be since your sister's time."

"Her tragedy?" asked Framton; somehow in this restful country spot tragedies seemed out of place.

"You may wonder why we keep that window wide open on an October afternoon," said the niece, indicating a large French window that opened onto a lawn.

"It is quite warm for the time of the year," said Framton; "but has that window got anything to do with the tragedy?"

"Out through that window, three years ago to a day, her husband and her two young brothers went off for their day's shooting. They never came back. In crossing the moor to their favourite snipe-shooting ground they were all three engulfed in a treacherous piece of bog. It had been that dreadful wet summer, you know, and places that were safe in other years gave way suddenly without warning. Their bodies were never recovered. That was the dreadful part of it." Here the child's voice lost its self-possessed note and became falteringly human. "Poor Aunt always thinks that they will come back some day, they and the little brown spaniel that was lost with them, and walk in at that window just as they used to do. That is why the window is kept open every evening till it is quite dusk. Poor dear Aunt, she has often told me how they went out, her husband with his white waterproof coat over his arm, and Ronnie, her youngest brother, singing, 'Bertie, why do you bound?' as he always did to tease her, because she said it got on her nerves. Do you know, sometimes on still, quiet evenings like this, I almost get a creepy feeling that they will all walk in through that window——"

She broke off with a little shudder. It was a relief to Framton when the aunt bustled into the room with a whirl of apologies for being late in making her appearance.

"I hope Vera has been amusing you?" she said.

"She has been very interesting," said Framton.

"I hope you don't mind the open window," said Mrs. Sappleton briskly; "my husband and brothers will be home directly from shooting, and they always come in this way. They've been out for snipe in the marshes today, so they'll make a fine mess over my poor carpets. So like you menfolk, isn't it?"

She rattled on cheerfully about the shooting and the scarcity of birds, and the prospects for duck in the winter. To Framton it was all purely horrible. He made a desperate but only partially successful effort to turn the talk onto a less ghastly topic; he was conscious that his hostess was giving him only a fragment of her attention, and her eyes were constantly straying past him to the open window and the lawn beyond. It was certainly an unfortunate coincidence that he should have paid his visit on this tragic anniversary.

"The doctors agree in ordering me complete rest, an absence of mental excitement, and avoidance of anything in the nature of violent physical exercise," announced Framton, who laboured under the tolerably widespread delusion that total strangers and chance acquaintances are hungry for the least detail of one's ailments and infirmities, their cause and cure. "On the matter of diet they are not so much in agreement," he continued.

"No?" said Mrs. Sappleton, in a voice which only replaced a yawn at the last moment. Then she suddenly brightened into alert attention—but not to what Framton was saying.

"Here they are at last!" she cried. "Just in time for tea, and don't they look as if they were muddy up to the eyes!"

Framton shivered slightly and turned towards the niece with a look intended to convey sympathetic comprehension. The child was staring out through the open window with dazed horror in her eyes. In a chill shock of nameless fear Framton swung round in his seat and looked in the same direction.

In the deepening twilight three figures were walking across the lawn towards the window; they all carried guns under their arms, and one of them was additionally burdened with a white coat hung over his shoulders. A tired brown spaniel kept close to their heels. Noiselessly they neared the house, and then a hoarse young voice chanted out of the dusk: "I said, Bertie, why do you bound?"

Framton grabbed wildly at his stick and hat; the hall door, the gravel drive, and the front gate were dimly noted stages in his headlong retreat. A cyclist coming along the road had to run into the hedge to avoid imminent collision.

"Here we are, my dear," said the bearer of the white mackintosh, coming in through the window; "fairly muddy, but most of it's dry. Who was that who bolted out as we came up?"

"A most extraordinary man, a Mr. Nuttel," said Mrs. Sappleton; "could only talk about his illnesses, and dashed off without a word of good-bye or apology when you arrived. One would think he had seen a ghost."

"I expect it was the spaniel," said the niece calmly; "he told me he had a horror of dogs. He was once hunted into a cemetery somewhere on the banks of the Ganges by a pack of pariah dogs, and had to spend the night in a newly dug grave with the creatures snarling and grinning and foaming just above him. Enough to make anyone lose their nerve."

Romance at short notice was her speciality.

The
Schartz-Metterklume
Method

LADY CARLOTTA stepped out onto the platform of the
small wayside station and took a turn or two up
and down its uninteresting length, to kill time till the
train should be pleased to proceed on its way. Then,
in the roadway beyond, she saw a horse struggling
with a more than ample load, and a carter of the sort
that seems to bear a sullen hatred against the animal
that helps him to earn a living. Lady Carlotta promptly betook her to the roadway, and put rather a different complexion on the struggle. Certain of her acquaintances were wont to give her plentiful admoni-
tion as to the undesirability of interfering on behalf
of a distressed animal, such interference being "none
of her business." Only once had she put the doctrine
of noninterference into practise, when one of its most
eloquent exponents had been besieged for nearly
three hours in a small and extremely uncomfortable
May tree by an angry boar pig, while Lady Carlotta,
on the other side of the fence, had proceeded with the
water-colour sketch she was engaged on, and refused

to interfere between the boar and his prisoner. It is to
be feared that she lost the friendship of the ultimately rescued lady. On this occasion she merely lost
the train, which gave way to the first sign of impatience it had shown throughout the journey, and
steamed off without her. She bore the desertion with
philosophical indifference; her friends and relations
were thoroughly well used to the fact of her luggage
arriving without her. She wired a vague noncommittal message to her destination to say that she was
coming on "by another train." Before she had time
to think what her next move might be, she was confronted by an imposingly attired lady, who seemed
to be taking a prolonged mental inventory of her
clothes and looks.

"You must be Miss Hope, the governess I've come
to meet," said the apparition, in a tone that admitted
of very little argument.

"Very well, if I must I must," said Lady Carlotta to
herself with dangerous meekness.

"I am Mrs. Quabarl," continued the lady; "and
where, pray, is your luggage?"

"It's gone astray," said the alleged governess, falling
in with the excellent rule of life that the absent are
always to blame; the luggage had, in point of fact, behaved with perfect correctitude. "I've just tele-
graphed about it," she added, with a nearer approach
to truth.

"How provoking," said Mrs. Quabarl; "these railway companies are so careless. However, my maid
can lend you things for the night," and she led the
way to her car.

During the drive to the Quabarl mansion Lady Carlotta was impressively introduced to the nature of the

charge that had been thrust upon her; she learned that Claude and Wilfrid were delicate, sensitive young people, that Irene had the artistic temperament highly developed, and that Viola was something or other else of a mould equally commonplace among children of that class and type in the twentieth century.

"I wish them not only to be *taught*," said Mrs. Quabarl, "but *interested* in what they learn. In their history lessons, for instance, you must try to make them feel that they are being introduced to the life stories of men and women who really lived, not merely committing a mass of names and dates to memory. French, of course, I shall expect you to talk at mealtimes several days in the week."

"I shall talk French four days of the week and Russian in the remaining three."

"Russian? My dear Miss Hope, no one in the house speaks or understands Russian."

"That will not embarrass me in the least," said Lady Carlotta coldly.

Mrs. Quabarl, to use a colloquial expression, was knocked off her perch. She was one of those imperfectly self-assured individuals who are magnificent and autocratic as long as they are not seriously opposed. The least show of unexpected resistance goes a long way towards rendering them cowed and apologetic. When the new governess failed to express wondering admiration of the large, newly purchased and expensive car, and lightly alluded to the superior advantages of one or two makes which had just been put on the market, the discomfiture of her patroness became almost abject. Her feelings were those which might have animated a general of ancient war-

faring days, on beholding his heaviest battle elephant
ignominiously driven off the field by slingers and
javelin throwers.

At dinner that evening, although reinforced by her
husband, who usually duplicated her opinions and
lent her moral support generally, Mrs. Quabarl re-
gained none of her lost ground. The governess not
only helped herself well and truly to wine, but held
forth with considerable show of critical knowledge on
various vintage matters, concerning which the Quabarls were in no wise able to pose as authorities. Previous governesses had limited their conversation on
the wine topic to a respectful and doubtless sincere
expression of a preference for water. When this one
went as far as to recommend a wine firm in whose
hands you could not go very far wrong Mrs. Quabarl
thought it time to turn the conversation into more
usual channels.

"We got very satisfactory references about you
from Canon Teep," she observed; "a very estimable
man, I should think."

"Drinks like a fish and beats his wife, otherwise a
very lovable character," said the governess imperturb-
ably.

"My *dear* Miss Hope! I trust you are exaggerat-
ing," exclaimed the Quabarls in unison.

"One must in justice admit that there is some prov-
ocation," continued the romancer. "Mrs. Teep is quite
the most irritating bridge player that I have ever
sat down with; her leads and declarations would con-
done a certain amount of brutality in her partner, but
to souse her with the contents of the only sodawater
syphon in the house on a Sunday afternoon, when
one couldn't get another, argues an indifference to

the comfort of others which I cannot altogether overlook. You may think me hasty in my judgments, but it was practically on account of the syphon incident that I left."

"We will talk of this some other time," said Mrs. Quabarl hastily.

"I shall never allude to it again," said the governess with decision.

Mr. Quabarl made a welcome diversion by asking what studies the new instructress proposed to inaugurate on the morrow.

"History to begin with," she informed him.

"Ah, history," he observed sagely; "now in teaching them history you must take care to interest them in what they learn. You must make them feel that they are being introduced to the life stories of men and women who really lived——"

"I've told her all that," interposed Mrs. Quabarl.

"I teach history on the Schartz-Metterklume method," said the governess loftily.

"Ah, yes," said her listeners, thinking it expedient to assume an acquaintance at least with the name.

"What are you children doing out here?" demanded Mrs. Quabarl the next morning, on finding Irene sitting rather glumly at the head of the stairs, while her sister was perched in an attitude of depressed discomfort on the window seat behind her, with a wolf-skin rug almost covering her.

"We are having a history lesson," came the unexpected reply. "I am supposed to be Rome, and Viola up there is the she-wolf; not a real wolf, but the figure of one that the Romans used to set store by—I forget why. Claude and Wilfrid have gone to fetch the shabby women."

"The shabby women?"

"Yes, they've got to carry them off. They didn't want to, but Miss Hope got one of father's fives bats and said she'd give them a number nine spanking if they didn't, so they've gone to do it."

A loud, angry screaming from the direction of the lawn drew Mrs. Quabarl thither in hot haste, fearful lest the threatened castigation might even now be in process of infliction. The outcry, however, came principally from the two small daughters of the lodge-keeper, who were being hauled and pushed towards the house by the panting and dishevelled Claude and Wilfrid, whose task was rendered even more arduous by the incessant, if not very effectual, attacks of the captured maidens' small brother. The governess, fives bat in hand, sat negligently on the stone balustrade, presiding over the scene with the cold impartiality of a Goddess of Battles. A furious and repeated chorus of "I'll tell Muvver" rose from the lodge children, but the lodge mother, who was hard of hearing, was for the moment immersed in the preoccupation of her washtub. After an apprehensive glance in the direction of the lodge (the good woman was gifted with the highly militant temper which is sometimes the privilege of deafness) Mrs. Quabarl flew indignantly to the rescue of the struggling captives.

"Wilfrid! Claude! Let those children go at once. Miss Hope, what on earth is the meaning of this scene?"

"Early Roman history; the Sabine women, don't you know? It's the Schartz-Metterklume method to make children understand history by acting it themselves; fixes it in their memory, you know. Of course, if, thanks to your interference, your boys go through life thinking that the Sabine women ultimately escaped, I really cannot be held responsible."

"You may be very clever and modern, Miss Hope," said Mrs. Quabarl firmly, "but I should like you to leave here by the next train. Your luggage will be sent after you as soon as it arrives."

"I'm not certain exactly where I shall be for the next few days," said the dismissed instructress of youth; "you might keep my luggage till I wire my address. There are only a couple of trunks and some golf clubs and a leopard cub."

"A leopard cub!" gasped Mrs. Quabarl. Even in her departure this extraordinary person seemed destined to leave a trail of embarrassment behind her.

"Well, it's rather left off being a cub; it's more than half-grown, you know. A fowl every day and a rabbit on Sundays is what it usually gets. Raw beef makes it too excitable. Don't trouble about getting the car for me, I'm rather inclined for a walk."

And Lady Carlotta strode out of the Quabarl horizon.

The advent of the genuine Miss Hope, who had made a mistake as to the day on which she was due to arrive, caused a turmoil which that good lady was quite unused to inspiring. Obviously the Quabarl family had been woefully befooled, but a certain amount of relief came with the knowledge.

"How tiresome for you, dear Carlotta," said her hostess, when the overdue guest ultimately arrived; "how very tiresome losing your train and having to stop overnight in a strange place."

"Oh, dear, no," said Lady Carlotta; "not at all tiresome—for me."

A Holiday Task

KENELM JERTON entered the dining hall of the Golden Galleon Hotel in the full crush of the luncheon hour. Nearly every seat was occupied, and small additional tables had been brought in, where floor space permitted, to accommodate late-comers, with the result that many of the tables were almost touching each other. Jerton was beckoned by a waiter to the only vacant table that was discernible, and took his seat with the uncomfortable and wholly groundless idea that nearly everyone in the room was staring at him. He was a youngish man of ordinary appearance, quiet of dress and unobtrusive of manner, and he could never wholly rid himself of the idea that a fierce light of public scrutiny beat on him as though he had been a notability or a supernut. After he had ordered his lunch there came the unavoidable interval of waiting, with nothing to do but to stare at the flower-vase on his table and to be stared at (in imagination) by several flappers, some maturer beings of the same sex, and a satirical-looking Jew. In order to carry off the situation with some appearance of unconcern he became spuriously interested in the contents of the flower-vase.

"What is the name of those roses, d'you know?"

he asked the waiter. The waiter was ready at all times to conceal his ignorance concerning items of the wine-list or menu; he was frankly ignorant as to the specific name of the roses.

"*Amy Silvester Partington,*" said a voice at Jerton's elbow.

The voice came from a pleasant-faced, well-dressed young woman who was sitting at a table that almost touched Jerton's. He thanked her hurriedly and nervously for the information, and made some inconsequent remark about the flowers.

"It is a curious thing," said the young woman, "that I should be able to tell you the name of those roses without an effort of memory, because if you were to ask me my name I should be utterly unable to give it to you."

Jerton had not harboured the least intention of extending his thirst for name labels to his neighbour. After her rather remarkable announcement, however, he was obliged to say something in the way of polite inquiry.

"Yes," answered the lady, "I suppose it is a case of partial loss of memory. I was in the train coming down here; my ticket told me that I had come from Victoria and was bound for this place. I had a couple of five-pound notes and a sovereign on me, no visiting cards or any other means of identification, and no idea as to who I am. I can only hazily recollect that I have a title; I am Lady Somebody—beyond that my mind is a blank."

"Hadn't you any luggage with you?" asked Jerton.

"That is what I didn't know. I knew the name of this hotel and made up my mind to come here, and when the hotel porter who meets the trains asked if I had any luggage I had to invent a dressing bag and dress basket; I could always pretend that they had gone astray. I gave him the name of Smith, and presently he emerged from a confused pile of luggage and passengers with a dressing bag and dress basket labelled Kestrel-Smith. I had to take them; I don't see what else I could have done."

Jerton said nothing, but he rather wondered what the lawful owner of the baggage would do.

"Of course it was dreadful arriving at a strange hotel with the name of Kestrel-Smith, but it would have been worse to have arrived without luggage. Anyhow, I hate causing trouble."

Jerton had visions of harassed railway officials and distraught Kestrel-Smiths, but he made no attempt to clothe his mental picture in words. The lady continued her story.

"Naturally, none of my keys would fit the things, but I told an intelligent page boy that I had lost my key ring, and he had the locks forced in a twinkling. Rather too intelligent, that boy; he will probably end in Dartmoor. The Kestrel-Smith toilet tools aren't up to much, but they are better than nothing."

"If you feel sure that you have a title," said Jerton, "why not get hold of a peerage and go right through it?"

"I tried that. I skimmed through the list of the House of Lords in *Whitaker*, but a mere printed string of names conveys awfully little to one, you know. If you were an army officer and had lost your identity you might pore over the Army List for months without finding out who you were. I'm going on another tack; I'm trying to find out by various little tests who I am *not*—that will narrow the range of uncertainty down a bit. You may have noticed, for instance, that I'm lunching principally off lobster Newburg."

Jerton had not ventured to notice anything of the sort.

"It's an extravagance, because it's one of the most expensive dishes on the menu, but at any rate it proves that I'm not Lady Starping; she never touches shellfish, and poor Lady Braddleshrub has no digestion at all; if I am *her* I shall certainly die in agony in the course of the afternoon, and the duty of finding out who I am will devolve on the press and the police and those sort of people; I shall be past caring. Lady Knewford doesn't know one rose from another and she hates men, so she wouldn't have spoken to you in any case; and Lady Mousehilton flirts with every man she meets—I haven't flirted with you, have I?"

Jerton hastily gave the required assurance.

"Well, you see," continued the lady, "that knocks four off the list at once."

"It'll be rather a lengthy process bringing the list down to one," said Jerton.

"Oh, but, of course, there are heaps of them that I couldn't possibly be—women who've got grandchildren or sons old enough to have celebrated their coming of age. I've only got to consider the ones about my own age. I tell you how you might help me this afternoon, if you don't mind; go through any of the back numbers of *Country Life* and those sort of papers that you can find in the smoking room, and see if you come across my portrait with infant son or anything of that sort. It won't take you ten minuts. I'll meet you in the lounge about teatime. Thanks awfully."

And the Fair Unknown, having graciously pressed Jerton into the search for her lost identity, rose and left the room. As she passed the young man's table she halted for a moment and whispered:

"Did you notice that I tipped the waiter a shilling? We can cross Lady Ulwight off the list; she would have died rather than do that."

At five o'clock Jerton made his way to the hotel lounge; he had spent a diligent but fruitless quarter of an hour among the illustrated weeklies in the smoking room. His new acquaintance was seated at a small tea table, with a waiter hovering in attendance.

"China tea or Indian?" she asked as Jerton came up.

"China, please, and nothing to eat. Have you discovered anything?"

"Only negative information. I'm not Lady Befnal. She disapproves dreadfully of any form of gambling, so when I recognized a well-known bookmaker in the hotel lobby I went and put a tenner on an unnamed filly by William the Third out of Mitrovitza for the three-fifteen race. I suppose the fact of the animal being nameless was what attracted me."

"Did it win?" asked Jerton.

"No, came in fourth, the most irritating thing a horse can do when you've backed it win or place. Anyhow, I know now that I'm not Lady Befnal."

"It seems to me that the knowledge was rather dearly bought," commented Jerton.

"Well, yes, it has rather cleared me out," admitted the identity seeker; "a florin is about all I've got left on me. The lobster Newburg made my lunch rather an expensive one, and, of course, I had to tip that boy for what he did to the Kestrel-Smith locks. I've got rather a useful idea, though. I feel certain that I belong to the Pivot Club; I'll go back to town and ask the hall porter there if there are any letters for me. He knows all the members by sight, and if there are any letters or telephone messages waiting for me, of course that will solve the problem. If he says there aren't any, I shall say: 'You know who I am, don't you?' so I'll find out anyway."

The plan seemed a sound one; a difficulty in its execution suggested itself to Jerton.

"Of course," said the lady, when he hinted at the obstacle, "there's my fare back to town, and my bill here and cabs and things. If you lend me three pounds that ought to see me through comfortably. Thanks ever so. Then there is the question of that luggage: I don't want to be saddled with that for the rest of my life. I'll have it brought down to the hall and you can pretend to mount guard over it while I'm writing a letter. Then I shall just slip away to the station, and you can wander off to the smoking room, and they can do what they like with the things. They'll advertise them after a bit and the owner can claim them."

Jerton acquiesced in the manoeuvre, and duly mounted guard over the luggage while its temporary owner slipped unobtrusively out of the hotel. Her departure was not, however, altogether unnoticed. Two gentlemen were strolling past Jerton, and one of them remarked to the other:

"Did you see that tall young woman in grey who went out just now? She is the Lady——"

His promenade carried him out of earshot at the critical moment when he was about to disclose the elusive identity. The Lady Who? Jerton could scarcely run after a total stranger, break into his conversation, and ask him for information concerning a chance passerby. Besides, it was desirable that he should keep up the appearance of looking after the luggage. In a minute or two, however, the important personage, the man who knew, came strolling back alone. Jerton summoned up all his courage and waylaid him.

"I think I heard you say you knew the lady who went out of the hotel a few minutes ago, a tall lady, dressed in grey. Excuse me for asking if you could tell me her name; I've been talking to her for half an hour; she—er—she knows all my people and seems to know me, so I suppose I've met her somewhere before, but I'm blest if I can put a name to her. Could you——?"

"Certainly. She's a Mrs. Stroope."

"*Mrs.?*" queried Jerton.

"Yes, she's the Lady Champion at golf in my part of the world. An awful good sort, and goes about a good deal in Society, but she has an awkward habit of losing her memory every now and then, and gets into all sorts of fixes. She's furious, too, if you make any allusion to it afterwards. Good day, sir."

The stranger passed on his way, and before Jerton had had time to assimilate his information he found his whole attention centred on an angry-looking lady who was making loud and fretful-seeming inquiries of the hotel clerks.

"Has any luggage been brought here from the station by mistake, a dress basket and dressing case, with the name Kestrel-Smith? It can't be traced anywhere. I saw it put in at Victoria, that I'll swear. Why—there *is* my luggage! and the locks have been tampered with!"

Jerton heard no more. He fled down to the Turkish bath, and stayed there for hours.

The Storyteller

IT was a hot afternoon, and the railway carriage correspondingly sultry, and the next stop was at Templecombe, nearly an hour ahead. The occupants of the carriage were a small girl, and a smaller girl, and a small boy. An aunt belonging to the children occupied one corner seat, and the farther corner seat on the opposite side was occupied by a bachelor who was a stranger to their party, but the small girls and the small boy emphatically occupied the compartment. Both the aunt and the children were conversational in a limited, persistent way, reminding one of the attentions of a housefly that refused to be discouraged. Most of the aunt's remarks seemed to begin with "Don't," and nearly all of the children's remarks began with "Why?" The bachelor said nothing out loud.

"Don't, Cyril, don't," exclaimed the aunt, as the small boy began smacking the cushions of the seat, producing a cloud of dust at each blow.

"Come and look out of the window," she added.

The child moved reluctantly to the window. "Why are those sheep being driven out of that field?" he asked.

"I expect they are being driven to another field

where there is more grass," said the aunt weakly.

"But there is lots of grass in that field," protested the boy; "there's nothing else but grass there. Aunt, there's lots of grass in that field."

"Perhaps the grass in the other field is better," suggested the aunt fatuously.

"Why is it better?" came the swift, inevitable question.

"Oh, look at those cows!" exclaimed the aunt. Nearly every field along the line had contained cows or bullocks, but she spoke as though she were drawing attention to a rarity.

"Why is the grass in the other field better?" persisted Cyril.

The frown on the bachelor's face was deepening to a scowl. He was a hard, unsympathetic man, the aunt decided in her mind. She was utterly unable to come to any satisfactory decision about the grass in the other field.

The smaller girl created a diversion by beginning to recite "On the Road to Mandalay." She only knew the first line, but she put her limited knowledge to the fullest possible use. She repeated the line over and over again in a dreamy but resolute and very audible voice; it seemed to the bachelor as though someone had had a bet with her that she could not repeat the line aloud two thousand times without stopping. Whoever it was who had made the wager was likely to lose his bet.

"Come over here and listen to a story," said the aunt, when the bachelor had looked twice at her and once at the communication cord.

The children moved listlessly towards the aunt's

end of the carriage. Evidently her reputation as a storyteller did not rank high in their estimation.

In a low, confidential voice, interrupted at frequent intervals by loud, petulant questions from her listeners, she began an unenterprising and deplorably uninteresting story about a little girl who was good, and made friends with everyone on account of her goodness, and was finally saved from a mad bull by a number of rescuers who admired her moral character.

"Wouldn't they have saved her if she hadn't been good?" demanded the bigger of the small girls. It was exactly the question that the bachelor had wanted to ask.

"Well, yes," admitted the aunt lamely, "but I don't think they would have run quite so fast to her help if they had not liked her so much."

"It's the stupidest story I've ever heard," said the bigger of the small girls, with immense conviction.

"I didn't listen after the first bit, it was so stupid," said Cyril.

The smaller girl made no actual comment on the story, but she had long ago recommenced a murmured repetition of her favourite line.

"You don't seem to be a success as a storyteller," said the bachelor suddenly from his corner.

The aunt bristled in instant defence at this unexpected attack.

"It's a very difficult thing to tell stories that children can both understand and appreciate," she said stiffly.

"I don't agree with you," said the bachelor.

"Perhaps *you* would like to tell them a story," was the aunt's retort.

"Tell us a story," demanded the bigger of the small girls.

"Once upon a time," began the bachelor, "there was a little girl called Bertha, who was extraordinarily good."

The children's momentarily aroused interest began at once to flicker; all stories seemed dreadfully alike, no matter who told them.

"She did all that she was told, she was always truthful, she kept her clothes clean, ate milk puddings as though they were jam tarts, learned her lessons perfectly, and was polite in her manners."

"Was she pretty?" asked the bigger of the small girls.

"Not as pretty as any of you," said the bachelor, "but she was horribly good."

There was a wave of reaction in favour of the story; the word horrible in connection with goodness was a novelty that commended itself. It seemed to introduce a ring of truth that was absent from the aunt's tales of infant life.

"She was so good," continued the bachelor, "that she won several medals for goodness, which she always wore, pinned onto her dress. There was a medal for obedience, another medal for punctuality, and a third for good behaviour. They were large metal medals and they clicked against one another as she walked. No other child in the town where she lived had as many as three medals, so everybody knew that she must be an extra-good child."

"Horribly good," quoted Cyril.

"Everybody talked about her goodness, and the Prince of the country got to hear about it, and he said that as she was so very good she might be allowed once a week to walk in his park, which was just outside the town. It was a beautiful park, and no children were ever allowed in it, so it was a great honour for Bertha to be allowed to go there."

"Were there any sheep in the park?" demanded Cyril.

"No," said the bachelor, "there were no sheep."

"Why weren't there any sheep?" came the inevitable question arising out of that answer.

The aunt permitted herself a smile, which might almost have been described as a grin.

"There were no sheep in the park," said the bachelor, "because the Prince's mother had once had a dream that her son would either be killed by a sheep or else by a clock falling on him. For that reason the Prince never kept a sheep in his park or a clock in his palace."

The aunt suppressed a gasp of admiration.

"Was the Prince killed by a sheep or by a clock?" asked Cyril.

"He is still alive, so we can't tell whether the dream will come true," said the bachelor unconcernedly; "anyway, there were no sheep in the park, but there were lots of little pigs running all over the place."

"What colour were they?"

"Black with white faces, white with black spots, black all over, grey with white patches, and some were white all over."

The storyteller paused to let a full idea of the park's treasures sink into the children's imaginations; then he resumed:

"Bertha was rather sorry to find that there were no flowers in the park. She had promised her aunts, with tears in her eyes, that she would not pick any of the kind Prince's flowers, and she had meant to keep her promise, so of course it made her feel silly to find that there were no flowers to pick."

"Why weren't there any flowers?"

"Because the pigs had eaten them all," said the bachelor promptly. "The gardeners had told the Prince that you couldn't have pigs and flowers, so he decided to have pigs and no flowers."

There was a murmur of approval at the excellence of the Prince's decision; so many people would have decided the other way.

"There were lots of other delightful things in the park. There were ponds with gold and blue and green fish in them, and trees with beautiful parrots that said clever things at a moment's notice, and hummingbirds that hummed all the popular tunes of the day. Bertha walked up and down and enjoyed herself immensely, and thought to herself: 'If I were not so extraordinarily good I should not have been allowed to come into this beautiful park and enjoy all that there is to be seen in it,' and her three medals clinked against one another as she walked and helped to remind her how very good she really was. Just then an enormous wolf came prowling into the park to see if it could catch a fat little pig for its supper."

"What colour was it?" asked the children, amid an immediate quickening of interest.

"Mud-colour all over, with a black tongue and pale grey eyes that gleamed with unspeakable ferocity. The first thing that it saw in the park was Bertha; her pinafore was so spotlessly white and clean that it could be seen from a great distance. Bertha saw the wolf and saw that it was stealing towards her, and she began to wish that she had never been allowed to come into the park. She ran as hard as she could, and the wolf came after her with huge leaps and bounds. She managed to reach a shrubbery of myrtle bushes and she hid herself in one of the thickest of the bushes. The wolf came sniffing among the branches, its black tongue lolling out of its mouth and its pale grey eyes glaring with rage. Bertha was terribly frightened, and thought to herself: 'If I had not been so extraordinarily good I should have been safe in the town at this moment.' However, the scent of the myrtle was so strong that the wolf could not sniff out where Bertha was hiding, and the bushes were so thick that he might have hunted about in them for a long time without catching sight of her, so he thought he might as well go off and catch a little pig instead. Bertha was trembling very much at having the wolf prowling and sniffing so near her, and as she trembled the medal for obedience clinked against the medals for good conduct and punctuality. The wolf was just moving away when he heard the sound of the medals clinking and stopped to listen; they clinked again in a bush quite near him. He dashed into the bush, his pale grey eyes gleaming with ferocity and triumph, and dragged Bertha out and devoured her to the last morsel. All that was left of her were her shoes, bits of clothing, and the three medals for goodness."

"Were any of the little pigs killed?"

"No, they all escaped."

"The story began badly," said the smaller of the small girls, "but it had a beautiful ending."

"It is the most beautiful story that I ever heard,"

said the bigger of the small girls, with immense decision.

"It is the *only* beautiful story I have ever heard," said Cyril.

A dissentient opinion came from the aunt.

"A most improper story to tell to young children! You have undermined the effect of years of careful teaching."

"At any rate," said the bachelor, collecting his belongings preparatory to leaving the carriage, "I kept them quiet for ten minutes, which was more than you were able to do."

"Unhappy woman!" he observed to himself as he walked down the platform of Templecombe station; "for the next six months or so those children will assail her in public with demands for an improper story!"

The Name Day

ADVENTURES, according to the proverb, are to the adventurous. Quite as often they are to the nonadventurous, to the retiring, to the constitutionally timid. John James Abbleway had been endowed by Nature with the sort of disposition that instinctively avoids Carlist intrigues, slum crusades, the tracking of wounded wild beasts, and the moving of hostile amendments at political meetings. If a mad dog or a Mad Mullah had come his way he would have surrendered the way without hesitation. At school he had unwillingly acquired a thorough knowledge of the German tongue out of deference to the plainly expressed wishes of a foreign-languages master, who, though he taught modern subjects, employed oldfashioned methods in driving his lessons home. It was this enforced familiarity with an important commercial language which thrust Abbleway in later years into strange lands where adventures were less easy to guard against than in the ordered atmosphere of an English country town. The firm that he worked for saw fit to send him one day on a prosaic business errand to the far city of Vienna, and, having sent him there, continued to keep him there, still engaged in humdrum affairs of commerce, but with the possibilities of romance and adventure, or even misadventure, jostling at his elbow. After two and a half years of exile, however, John James Abbleway had embarked on only one hazardous undertaking, and that was of a nature which would assuredly have overtaken him sooner or later if he had been leading a sheltered, stay-at-home existence at Dorking or Huntingdon. He fell placidly in love with a placidly lovable English girl, the sister of one of his commercial colleagues, who was improving her mind by a short trip to foreign parts, and in due course he was formally accepted as the young man she was engaged to. The further step by which she was to become Mrs. John Abbleway was to take place a twelvemonth hence in a town in the English midlands, by which time the firm that employed John James would have no further need for his presence in the Austrian capital.

It was early in April, two months after the installation of Abbleway as the young man Miss Penning was engaged to, when he received a letter from her, written from Venice. She was still peregrinating under the wing of her brother, and as the latter's business arrangements would take him across to Fiume for a day or two, she had conceived the idea that it would be rather jolly if John could obtain leave of absence and run down to the Adriatic coast to meet them. She had looked up the route on the map, and the journey did not appear likely to be expensive. Between the lines of her communication there lay a hint that if he really cared for her——

Abbleway obtained leave of absence and added a journey to Fiume to his life's adventures. He left Vienna on a cold, cheerless day. The flower shops were full of spring blooms, and the weekly organs of illustrated humour were full of spring topics, but the skies were heavy with clouds that looked like cotton wool that has been kept overlong in a shop window.

"Snow comes," said the train official to the station officials, and they agreed that snow was about to come. And it came, rapidly, plenteously. The train had not been more than an hour on its journey when the cotton-wool clouds commenced to dissolve in a blinding downpour of snowflakes. The forest trees on either side of the line were speedily coated with a heavy white mantle, the telegraph wires became thick glistening ropes, the line itself was buried more and more completely under a carpeting of snow, through which the not very powerful engine ploughed its way with increasing difficulty. The Vienna-Fiume line is scarcely the best equipped of the Austrian State railways, and Abbleway began to have serious fears for a breakdown. The train had slowed down to a painful and precarious crawl and presently came to a halt at a spot where the drifting snow had accumulated in a formidable barrier. The engine made a special effort and broke through the obstruction, but in the course of another twenty minutes it was again held up. The process of breaking through was renewed and the train doggedly resumed its way, encountering and surmounting fresh hindrances at frequent intervals. After a standstill of unusually long duration in a particularly deep drift, the compartment in which Abbleway was sitting gave a huge jerk and a lurch, and then seemed to remain stationary; it undoubtedly was not moving, and yet he could hear the puffing of the engine and the slow rumbling and jolting of wheels. The puffing and rumbling grew fainter, as though it were dying away through the agency of intervening distance. Abbleway suddenly gave vent to an exclamation of scandalized alarm, opened the window, and peered out into the snowstorm. The flakes perched on his eyelashes and blurred his vision, but he saw enough to help him to realize what had happened. The engine had made a mighty plunge through the drift and had gone merrily forward, lightened of the load of its rear carriage, whose coupling had snapped under the strain. Abbleway was alone, or almost alone, with a derelict railway waggon, in the heart of some Styrian or Croatian forest. In the third-class compartment next to his own he remembered to have seen a peasant woman, who had entered the train at a small wayside station. "With the exception of that woman," he exclaimed dramatically to himself, "the nearest living beings are probably a pack of wolves."

Before making his way to the third-class compartment to acquaint his fellow traveller with the extent of the disaster, Abbleway hurriedly pondered the question of the woman's nationality. He had acquired a smattering of Slavonic tongues during his residence in Vienna, and felt competent to grapple with several racial possibilities.

"If she is Croat or Serb or Bosniak I shall be able to make her understand," he promised himself. "If she is Magyar, heaven help me! We shall have to converse entirely by signs."

He entered the carriage and made his momentous announcement in the best approach to Croat speech that he could achieve.

"The train has broken away and left us!"

The woman shook her head with a movement that

might be intended to convey resignation to the will of heaven, but probably meant noncomprehension. Abbleway repeated his information with variations of Slavonic tongues and generous display of pantomime.

"Ah," said the woman at last in German dialect, "the train has gone? We are left. Ah, so."

She seemed about as much interested as though Abbleway had told her the result of the municipal elections in Amsterdam.

"They will find out at some station, and when the line is clear of snow they will send an engine. It happens that way sometimes."

"We may be here all night!" exclaimed Abbleway.

The woman looked as though she thought it possible.

"Are there wolves in these parts?" asked Abbleway hurriedly.

"Many," said the woman; "just outside this forest my aunt was devoured three years ago, as she was coming home from market. The horse and a young pig that was in the cart were eaten too. The horse was a very old one, but it was a beautiful young pig, oh, so fat. I cried when I heard that it was taken. They spare nothing."

"They may attack us here," said Abbleway tremulously; "they could easily break in, these carriages are like matchwood. We may both be devoured."

"You, perhaps," said the woman calmly; "not me."

"Why not you?" demanded Abbleway.

"It is the day of St. Mariä Kleophä, my name day. She would not allow me to be eaten by wolves on her

day. Such a thing could not be thought of. You, yes,
but not me."

Abbleway changed the subject.

"It is only afternoon now; if we are to be left here
till morning we shall be starving."

"I have here some good eatables," said the woman
tranquilly; on my festival day it is natural that I
should have provision with me. I have five good blood
sausages; in the town shops they cost twenty-five heller each. Things are dear in the town shops."

"I will give you fifty heller apiece for a couple of
them," said Abbleway with some enthusiasm.

"In a railway accident things become very dear,"
said the woman; "these blood sausages are four
kronen apiece."

"Four kronen!" exclaimed Abbleway; "four kronen
for a blood sausage!"

"You cannot get them any cheaper on this train,"
said the woman, with relentless logic, "because there
aren't any others to get. In Agram you can buy them
cheaper, and in Paradise no doubt they will be given
to us for nothing, but here they cost four kronen each.
I have a small piece of Emmenthaler cheese and a
honey cake and a piece of bread that I can let you
have. That will be another three kronen, eleven kron-
en in all. There is a piece of ham, but that I cannot
let you have on my name day."

Abbleway wondered to himself what price she
would have put on the ham, and hurried to pay her
the eleven kronen before her emergency tariff ex-
panded into a famine tariff. As he was taking possession of his modest store of eatables he suddenly heard
a noise which set his heart thumping in a miserable
fever of fear. There was a scraping and shuffling as of

some animal or animals trying to climb up to the footboard. In another moment, through the snow-encrusted glass of the carriage window, he saw a gaunt prick-eared head, with gaping jaw and lolling tongue and gleaming teeth; a second later another head shot up.

"There are hundreds of them," whispered Abbleway; "they have scented us. They will tear the carriage to pieces. We shall be devoured."

"Not me, on my name day. The holy Mariä Kleophä would not permit it," said the woman with provoking calm.

The heads dropped down from the window and an uncanny silence fell on the beleaguered carriage. Abbleway neither moved nor spoke. Perhaps the brutes had not clearly seen or winded the human occupants of the carriage, and had prowled away on some other errand of rapine.

The long torture-laden minutes passed slowly away.

"It grows cold," said the woman suddenly, crossing over to the far end of the carriage, where the heads had appeared. "The heating apparatus does not work any longer. See, over there beyond the trees, there is a chimney with smoke coming from it. It is not far, and the snow has nearly stopped. I shall find a path through the forest to that house with the chimney."

"But the wolves!" exclaimed Abbleway; "they may——"

"Not on my name day," said the woman obstinately, and before he could stop her she had opened the door and climbed down into the snow. A moment later he hid his face in his hands; two gaunt lean figures rushed upon her from the forest. No doubt she had courted her fate, but Abbleway had no wish to see a human being torn to pieces and devoured before his eyes.

When he looked at last a new sensation of scandalized astonishment took possession of him. He had been straitly brought up in a small English town, and he was not prepared to be the witness of a miracle. The wolves were not doing anything worse to the woman than drench her with snow as they gambolled round her.

A short, joyous bark revealed the clue to the situation.

"Are those—dogs?" he called weakly.

"My cousin Karl's dogs, yes," she answered; "that is his inn, over beyond the trees. I knew it was there, but I did not want to take you there; he is always grasping with strangers. However, it grows too cold to remain in the train. Ah, ah, see what comes!"

A whistle sounded, and a relief engine made its appearance, snorting its way sulkily through the snow. Abbleway did not have the opportunity for finding out whether Karl was really avaricious.

The Lumber Room

THE CHILDREN were to be driven, as a special treat, to the sands at Jagborough. Nicholas was not to be of the party; he was in disgrace. Only that morning he had refused to eat his wholesome bread and milk on the seemingly frivolous ground that there was a frog in it. Older and wiser and better people had told him that there could not possibly be a frog in his bread and milk and that he was not to talk nonsense; he continued, nevertheless, to talk what seemed the veriest nonsense, and described with much detail the colouration and markings of the alleged frog. The dramatic part of the incident was that there really was a frog in Nicholas' basin of bread and milk; he had put it there himself, so he felt entitled to know something about it. The sin of taking a frog from the garden and putting it into a bowl of wholesome bread and milk was enlarged on at great length, but the fact that stood out clearest in the whole affair, as it presented itself to the mind of Nicholas, was that the older, wiser, and better people had been proved to be profoundly in error in matters about which they had expressed the utmost assurance.

"You said there couldn't possibly be a frog in my bread and milk; there *was* a frog in my bread and milk," he repeated, with the insistence of a skilled tactician who does not intend to shift from favourable ground.

So his boy cousin and girl cousin and his quite uninteresting younger brother were to be taken to Jagborough sands that afternoon and he was to stay at home. His cousins' aunt, who insisted, by an unwarranted stretch of imagination, in styling herself his aunt also, had hastily invented the Jagborough expedition in order to impress on Nicholas the delights that he had justly forfeited by his disgraceful conduct at the breakfast table. It was her habit, whenever one of the children fell from grace, to improvise something of a festival nature from which the offender would be rigourously debarred; if all the children sinned collectively they were suddenly informed of a circus in a neighbouring town, a circus of unrivalled merit and uncounted elephants, to which, but for their depravity, they would have been taken that very day.

A few decent tears were looked for on the part of Nicholas when the moment for the departure of the expedition arrived. As a matter of fact, however, all the crying was done by his girl cousin, who scraped her knee rather painfully against the step of the carriage as she was scrambling in.

"How she did howl," said Nicholas cheerfully, as the party drove off without any of the elation of high spirits that should have characterized it.

"She'll soon get over that," said the *soi-disant* aunt; "it will be a glorious afternoon for racing about over those beautiful sands. How they will enjoy themselves."

"Bobby won't enjoy himself much, and he won't

race much either," said Nicholas with a grim chuckle; "his boots are hurting him. They're too tight."

"Why didn't he tell me they were hurting?" asked the aunt with some asperity.

"He told you twice, but you weren't listening. You often don't listen when we tell you important things."

"You are not to go into the gooseberry garden," said the aunt, changing the subject.

"Why not?" demanded Nicholas.

"Because you are in disgrace," said the aunt loftily.

Nicholas did not admit the flawlessness of the reasoning; he felt perfectly capable of being in disgrace and in a gooseberry garden at the same moment. His face took on an expression of considerable obstinacy. It was clear to his aunt that he was determined to get into the gooseberry garden, "only," as she remarked to herself, "because I have told him he is not to."

Now the gooseberry garden had two doors by which it might be entered, and once a small person like Nicholas could slip in there he could effectually disappear from view amid the masking growth of artichokes, raspberry canes, and fruit bushes. The aunt had many other things to do that afternoon, but she spent an hour or two in trivial gardening operations among flower beds and shrubberies, whence she could keep a watchful eye on the two doors that led to the forbidden paradise. She was a woman of few ideas, with immense powers of concentration.

Nicholas made one or two sorties into the front garden, wriggling his way with obvious stealth of purpose towards one or other of the doors, but never able for a moment to evade the aunt's watchful eye. As a matter of fact, he had no intention of trying to get into the gooseberry garden, but it was extremely con-

venient for him that his aunt should believe that he
had; it was a belief that would keep her on self-im-
posed sentry duty for the greater part of the afternoon. Having thoroughly confirmed and fortified her
suspicions, Nicholas slipped back into the house and
rapidly put into execution a plan of action that had
long germinated in his brain. By standing on a chair
in the library one could reach a shelf on which re-
posed a fat, important-looking key. The key was as
important as it looked; it was the instrument which
kept the mysteries of the lumber room secure from
unauthorized intrusion, which opened a way only for
aunts and suchlike privileged persons. Nicholas had
not had much experience of the art of fitting keys into
keyholes and turning locks, but for some days past he
had practised with the key of the schoolroom door; he
did not believe in trusting too much to luck and accident. The key turned stiffly in the lock, but it turned.
The door opened, and Nicholas was in an unknown
land, compared with which the gooseberry garden
was a stale delight, a mere material pleasure.

Often and often Nicholas had pictured to himself
what the lumber room might be like, that region that
was so carefully sealed from youthful eyes and concerning which no questions were ever answered. It
came up to his expectations. In the first place it was
large and dimly lit, one high window opening onto
the forbidden garden being its only source of illumi-
nation. In the second place it was a storehouse of un-
imagined treasures. The aunt-by-assertion was one of
those people who think that things spoil by use and
consign them to dust and damp by way of preserving
them. Such parts of the house as Nicholas knew best
were rather bare and cheerless, but here there were

wonderful things for the eye to feast on. First and foremost there was a piece of framed tapestry that was evidently meant to be a fire screen. To Nicholas it was a living, breathing story; he sat down on a roll of Indian hangings, glowing in wonderful colours beneath a layer of dust, and took in all the details of the tapestry picture. A man, dressed in the hunting costume of some remote period, had just transfixed a stag with an arrow; it could not have been a difficult shot because the stag was only one or two paces away from him; in the thickly growing vegetation that the picture suggested it would not have been difficult to creep up to a feeding stag, and the two spotted dogs that were springing forward to join in the chase had evidently been trained to keep to heel till the arrow was discharged. That part of the picture was simple, if interesting, but did the huntsman see, what Nicholas saw, that four galloping wolves were coming in his direction through the wood? There might be more than four of them hidden behind the trees, and in any case would the man and his dogs be able to cope with the four wolves if they made an attack? The man had only two arrows left in his quiver, and he might miss with one or both of them; all one knew about his skill in shooting was that he could hit a large stag at a ridiculously short range. Nicholas sat for many golden minutes revolving the possibilities of the scene; he was inclined to think that there were more than four wolves and that the man and his dogs were in a tight corner.

But there were other objects of delight and interest claiming his instant attention; there were quaint twisted candlesticks in the shape of snakes, and a teapot fashioned like a china duck, out of whose open

beak the tea was supposed to come. How dull and
shapeless the nursery teapot seemed in comparison!
And there was a carved sandalwood box packed tight
with aromatic cotton wool, and between the layers of
cotton wool were little brass figures, hump-necked
bulls, and peacocks and goblins, delightful to see
and to handle. Less promising in appearance was a
large square book with plain black covers; Nicholas
peeped into it, and, behold, it was full of coloured
pictures of birds. And such birds! In the garden, and
in the lanes when he went for a walk, Nicholas came
across a few birds, of which the largest were an occasional magpie or wood pigeon; here were herons and
bustards, kites, toucans, tiger bitterns, brush turkeys,
ibises, golden pheasants, a whole portrait gallery of
undreamed-of creatures. And as he was admiring the
colouring of the mandarin duck and assigning a life
history to it, the voice of his aunt in shrill vociferation
of his name came from the gooseberry garden without. She had grown suspicious at his long disappearance, and had leapt to the conclusion that he had
climbed over the wall behind the sheltering screen of
the lilac bushes; she was now engaged in energetic
and rather hopeless search for him among the artichokes and raspberry canes.

"Nicholas, Nicholas!" she screamed, "you are to
come out of this at once. It's no use trying to hide
there; I can see you all the time."

It was probably the first time for twenty years that
anyone had smiled in that lumber room.

Presently the angry repetitions of Nicholas' name
gave way to a shriek, and a cry for somebody to come
quickly. Nicholas shut the book, restored it carefully
to its place in a corner, and shook some dust from a

neighbouring pile of newspapers over it. Then he crept from the room, locked the door, and replaced the key exactly where he had found it. His aunt was still calling his name when he sauntered into the front garden.

"Who's calling?" he asked.

"Me," came the answer from the other side of the wall; "didn't you hear me? I've been looking for you in the gooseberry garden, and I've slipped into the rain-water tank. Luckily there's no water in it, but the sides are slippery and I can't get out. Fetch the little ladder from under the cherry tree——"

"I was told I wasn't to go into the gooseberry garden," said Nicholas promptly.

"I told you not to, and now I tell you that you may," came the voice from the rain-water tank, rather impatiently.

"Your voice doesn't sound like Aunt's," objected Nicholas; "you may be the Evil One tempting me to be disobedient. Aunt often tells me that the Evil One tempts me and that I always yield. This time I'm not going to yield."

"Don't talk nonsense," said the prisoner in the tank; "go and fetch the ladder."

"Will there be strawberry jam for tea?" asked Nicholas innocently.

"Certainly there will be," said the aunt, privately resolving that Nicholas should have none of it.

"Now I know that you are the Evil One and not Aunt," shouted Nicholas gleefully; "when we asked Aunt for strawberry jam yesterday she said there wasn't any. I know there are four jars of it in the store cupboard, because I looked, and of course you know it's there, but *she* doesn't, because she said there wasn't any. Oh, Devil, you *have* sold yourself!"

There was an unusual sense of luxury in being able to talk to an aunt as though one was talking to the Evil One, but Nicholas knew, with childish discernment, that such luxuries were not to be overindulged in. He walked noisily away, and it was a kitchenmaid, in search of parsley, who eventually rescued the aunt from the rain-water tank.

Tea that evening was partaken of in a fearsome silence. The tide had been at its highest when the children had arrived at Jagborough Cove, so there had been no sands to play on—a circumstance that the aunt had overlooked in the haste of organizing her punitive expedition. The tightness of Bobby's boots had had disastrous effect on his temper the whole of the afternoon, and altogether the children could not have been said to have enjoyed themselves. The aunt maintained the frozen muteness of one who has suffered undignified and unmerited detention in a rain-water tank for thirty-five minutes. As for Nicholas, he, too, was silent, in the absorption of one who has much to think about; it was just possible, he considered, that the huntsman would escape with his hounds while the wolves feasted on the stricken stag.

The Disappearance of
Crispina Umberleigh

IN A FIRST-CLASS CARRIAGE of a train speeding Balk-
anward across the flat, green Hungarian plain,
two Britons sat in friendly, fitful converse. They had
first foregathered in the cold grey dawn at the
frontier line, where the presiding eagle takes on an
extra head and Teuton lands pass from Hohenzollern
to Habsburg keeping—and where a probing official
beak requires to delve in polite and perhaps perfunc-
tory, but always tiresome, manner into the baggage
of sleep-hungry passengers. After a day's break of
their journey at Vienna the travellers had again foregathered at the trainside and paid one another the
compliment of settling instinctively into the same
carriage. The elder of the two had the appearance
and manner of a diplomat; in point of fact he was
the well-connected foster brother of a wine business.
The other was certainly a journalist. Neither man was
talkative and each was grateful to the other for not
being talkative. That is why from time to time they
talked.

One topic of conversation naturally thrust itself
forward in front of all others. In Vienna the pre-

vious day they had learned of the mysterious vanishing of a world-famous picture from the walls of the Louvre.

"A dramatic disappearance of that sort is sure to produce a crop of imitations," said the Journalist.

"It has had a lot of anticipations, for the matter of that," said the Wine Brother.

"Oh, of course there have been thefts from the Louvre before."

"I was thinking of the spiriting away of human beings rather than pictures. In particular I was thinking of the case of my aunt, Crispina Umberleigh."

"I remember hearing something of the affair," said the Journalist, "but I was away from England at the time. I never quite knew what was supposed to have happened."

"You may hear what really happened if you will respect it as a confidence," said the Wine Merchant. "In the first place I may say that the disappearance of Mrs. Umberleigh was not regarded by the family entirely as a bereavement. My uncle, Edward Umberleigh, was not by any means a weak-kneed individual, in fact in the world of politics he had to be reckoned with more or less as a strong man, but he was unmistakably dominated by Crispina; indeed, I never met any human being who was not frozen into subjection when brought into prolonged contact with her. Some people are born to command; Crispina (Mrs. Umberleigh) was born to legislate, codify, administrate, censor, license, ban, execute, and sit in judgment generally. If she was not born with that destiny she adopted it at an early age. From the kitchen regions upwards everyone in the household came under her despotic sway and stayed there with the submissiveness of molluscs involved in a glacial epoch. As a nephew on a footing of only occasional visits she affected me merely as an epidemic, disagreeable while it lasted, but without any permanent effect; but her own sons and daughters stood in mortal awe of her; their studies, friendships, diet, amusements, religious observances, and ways of doing their hair were all regulated and ordained according to the august lady's will and pleasure. This will help you to understand the sensation of stupefaction which was caused in the family when she unobtrusively and inexplicably vanished. It was as though St. Paul's Cathedral or the Piccadilly Hotel had disappeared in the night, leaving nothing but an open space to mark where it had stood. As far as was known nothing was troubling her; in fact there was much before her to make life particularly well worth living. The youngest boy had come back from school with an unsatisfactory report, and she was to have sat in judgment on him the very afternoon of the day she disappeared—if it had been he who had vanished in a hurry one could have supplied the motive. Then she was in the middle of a newspaper correspondence with a rural dean in which she had already proved him guilty of heresy, inconsistency, and unworthy quibbling, and no ordinary consideration would have induced her to discontinue the controversy. Of course the matter was put in the hands of the police, but as far as possible it was kept out of the papers, and the generally accepted explanation of her withdrawal from her social circle was that she had gone into a nursing home."

"And what was the immediate effect on the home circle?" asked the Journalist.

"All the girls bought themselves bicycles; the feminine cycling craze was still in existence, and Crispina had rigidly vetoed any participation in it among the members of her household. The youngest boy let himself go to such an extent during his next term that it had to be his last as far as that particular establishment was concerned. The elder boys propounded a theory that their mother might be wandering somewhere abroad, and searched for her assiduously, chiefly, it must be admitted, in a class of Montmartre resort where it was extremely improbable that she would be found."

"And all this while couldn't your uncle get hold of the least clue?"

"As a matter of fact he had received some information, though of course I did not know of it at the time. He got a message one day telling him that his wife had been kidnapped and smuggled out of the country; she was said to be hidden away, in one of the islands off the coast of Norway I think it was, in comfortable surroundings and well cared for. And with the information came a demand for money; a lump sum was to be handed over to her kidnappers, and a further sum of £2,000 was to be paid yearly. Failing this, she would be immediately restored to her family."

The Journalist was silent for a moment and then began to laugh quietly.

"It was certainly an inverted form of holding for ransom," he said.

"If you had known my aunt," said the Wine Merchant, "you would have wondered that they didn't put the figure higher."

"I realize the temptation. Did your uncle succumb to it?"

"Well, you see, he had to think of others as well as himself. For the family to have gone back into the Crispina thraldom after having tasted the delights of liberty would have been a tragedy, and there were even wider considerations to be taken into account. Since his bereavement he had unconsciously taken up a far bolder and more initiatory line in public affairs, and his popularity and influence had increased correspondingly. From being merely a strong man in the political world he began to be spoken of as *the* strong man. All this he knew would be jeopardized if he once more dropped into the social position of the husband of Mrs. Umberleigh. He was a rich man, and the £2,000 a year, though not exactly a fleabite, did not seem an extravagant price to pay for the boarding-out of Crispina. Of course, he had severe qualms of conscience about the arrangement. Later on, when he took me into his confidence, he told me that in paying the ransom, or hush money as I should have called it, he was partly influenced by the fear that if he refused it the kidnappers might have vented their rage and disappointment on their captive. It was better, he said, to think of her being well cared for as a highly valued paying guest in one of the Lofoden Islands than to have her struggling miserably home in a maimed and mutilated condition. Anyway he paid the yearly instalment as punctually as one pays a fire insurance, and with equal promptitude there would come an acknowledgment of the money and a brief statement to the effect that Crispina was in good health and fairly cheerful spirits. One report even mentioned that she was busying herself with a scheme for proposed reforms in church management to be pressed on the local pastorate. Another spoke of a rheumatic attack and a journey to a 'cure' on the mainland, and on that occasion an additional eighty pounds was demanded and conceded. Of course it was to the interest of the kidnappers to keep their charge in good health, but the secrecy with which they managed to shroud their arrangements argued a really wonderful organization. If my uncle was paying a rather high price, at least he could console himself with the reflection that he was paying specialists' fees."

"Meanwhile had the police given up all attempts to track the missing lady?" asked the Journalist.

"Not entirely; they came to my uncle from time to time to report on clues which they thought might yield some elucidation as to her fate or whereabouts, but I think they had their suspicions that he was possessed of more information than he had put at their disposal. And then, after a disappearance of more than eight years, Crispina returned with dramatic suddenness to the home she had left so mysteriously."

"She had given her captors the slip?"

"She had never been captured. Her wandering away had been caused by a sudden and complete loss of memory. She usually dressed rather in the style of a superior kind of charwoman, and it was not so very surprising that she should have imagined that she was one, and still less that people should accept her statement and help her to get work. She had wandered as far afield as Birmingham, and found fairly steady employment there, her energy and en-

thusiasm in putting people's rooms in order coun-
terbalancing her obstinate and domineering charac-
teristics. It was the shock of being patronizingly ad-
dressed as 'my good woman' by a curate, who was
disputing with her where the stove should be placed
in a parish concert hall, that led to the sudden res-
toration of her memory. 'I think you forget who you
are speaking to,' she observed crushingly, which was
rather unduly severe, considering she had only just
remembered it herself."

"But," exclaimed the Journalist, "the Lofoden Is-
land people! Who had they got hold of?"

"A purely mythical prisoner. It was an attempt
in the first place by someone who knew something
of the domestic situation, probably a discharged va-
let, to bluff a lump sum out of Edward Umberleigh
before the missing woman turned up; the subsequent
yearly instalments were an unlooked-for increment
to the original haul.

"Crispina found that the eight years' interregnum
had materially weakened her ascendency over her
now grown-up offspring. Her husband, however,
never accomplished anything great in the political
world after her return; the strain of trying to account
satisfactorily for an unspecified expenditure of
£16,000 spread over eight years sufficiently occupied his mental energies. Here is Belgrad and another
custom house."

The Wolves of Cernogratz

"ARE THERE any old legends attached to the castle?" asked Conrad of his sister. Conrad was a prosperous Hamburg merchant, but he was the one poetically dispositioned member of an eminently practical family.

The Baroness Gruebel shrugged her plump shoulders.

"There are always legends hanging about these old places. They are not difficult to invent and they cost nothing. In this case there is a story that when any one dies in the castle all the dogs in the village and the wild beasts in the forest howl the night long. It would not be pleasant to listen to, would it?"

"It would be weird and romantic," said the Hamburg merchant.

"Anyhow, it isn't true," said the Baroness complacently; "since we bought the place we have had proof that nothing of the sort happens. When the old mother-in-law died last springtime we all listened, but there was no howling. It is just a story that lends dignity to the place without costing anything."

"The story is not as you have told it," said Amalie, the grey old governess. Everyone turned and looked at her in astonishment. She was wont to sit silent and prim and faded in her place at table, never speaking unless someone spoke to her, and there were few who troubled themselves to make conversation with her. Today a sudden volubility had descended on her; she continued to talk, rapidly and nervously, looking straight in front of her and seeming to address no one in particular.

"It is not when *anyone* dies in the castle that the howling is heard. It was when one of the Cernogratz family died here that the wolves came from far and near and howled at the edge of the forest just before the death hour. There were only a few wolves that had their lairs in this part of the forest, but at such a time the keepers say there would be scores of them, gliding about in the shadows and howling in chorus, and the dogs of the castle and the village and all the farms round would bay and howl in fear and anger at the wolf chorus, and as the soul of the dying one left its body a tree would crash down in the park. That is what happened when a Cernogratz died in his family castle. But for a stranger dying here, of course no wolf would howl and no tree would fall. Oh, no."

There was a note of defiance, almost of contempt, in her voice as she said the last words. The well-fed, much-too-well-dressed Baroness stared angrily at the dowdy old woman who had come forth from her usual and seemly position of effacement to speak so disrespectfully.

"You seem to know quite a lot about the von Cernogratz legends, Fraulein Schmidt," she said sharply; "I did not know that family histories were among the subjects you are supposed to be proficient in."

The answer to her taunt was even more unexpected and astonishing than the conversational outbreak which had provoked it.

"I am a von Cernogratz myself," said the old woman, "that is why I know the family history."

"You a von Cernogratz? You!" came in an incredulous chorus.

"When we became very poor," she explained, "and I had to go out and give teaching lessons, I took another name; I thought it would be more in keeping. But my grandfather spent much of his time as a boy in this castle, and my father used to tell me many stories about it, and, of course, I knew all the family legends and stories. When one has nothing left to one but memories, one guards and dusts them with especial care. I little thought when I took service with you that I should one day come with you to the old home of my family. I could wish it had been anywhere else."

There was silence when she finished speaking, and then the Baroness turned the conversation to a less embarrassing topic than family histories. But afterwards, when the old governess had slipped away quietly to her duties, there arose a clamour of derision and disbelief.

"It was an impertinence," snapped out the Baron, his protruding eyes taking on a scandalized expression; "fancy the woman talking like that at our table. She almost told us we were nobodies, and I don't believe a word of it. She is just a Schmidt and nothing more. She has been talking to some of the peasants about the old Cernogratz family, and raked up their history and their stories."

"She wants to make herself out of some conse-

quence," said the Baroness; "she knows she will soon
be past work and she wants to appeal to our sym-
pathies. Her grandfather, indeed!"

The Baroness had the usual number of grandfa-
thers, but she never, never boasted about them.

"I dare say her grandfather was a pantry boy or
something of the sort in the castle," sniggered the
Baron; "that part of the story may be true."

The merchant from Hamburg said nothing; he had
seen tears in the old woman's eyes when she spoke
of guarding her memories—or, being of an imagina-
tive disposition, he thought he had.

"I shall give her notice to go as soon as the New
Year festivities are over," said the Baroness; "till
then I shall be too busy to manage without her."

But she had to manage without her all the same,
for in the cold biting weather after Christmas, the
old governness fell ill and kept to her room.

"It is most provoking," said the Baroness, as her
guests sat round the fire on one of the last evenings
of the dying year; "all the time that she has been
with us I cannot remember that she was ever seriously ill, too ill to go about and do her work, I mean.
And now, when I have the house full, and she could
be useful in so many ways, she goes and breaks
down. One is sorry for her, of course, she looks so
withered and shrunken, but it is intensely annoying
all the same."

"Most annoying," agreed the banker's wife sym-
pathetically; "it is the intense cold, I expect, it breaks
the old people up. It has been unusually cold this
year."

"The frost is the sharpest that has been known in
December for many years," said the Baron.

"And, of course, she is quite old," said the Baroness; "I wish I had given her notice some weeks ago, then she would have left before this happened to her.

Why, Wappi, what is the matter with you?"

The small, woolly lapdog had leapt suddenly down from its cushion and crept shivering under the sofa. At the same moment an outburst of angry barking came from the dogs in the castle yard, and other dogs could be heard yapping and barking in the distance.

"What is disturbing the animals?" asked the Baron.

And then the humans, listening intently, heard the sound that had roused the dogs to their demonstrations of fear and rage; heard a long-drawn whining howl, rising and falling, seeming at one moment leagues away, at others sweeping across the snow until it appeared to come from the foot of the castle walls. All the starved, cold misery of a frozen world, all the relentless hunger-fury of the wild, blended with other forlorn and haunting melodies to which one could give no name, seemed concentrated in that wailing cry.

"Wolves!" cried the Baron.

Their music broke forth in one raging burst, seeming to come from everywhere.

"Hundreds of wolves," said the Hamburg merchant, who was a man of strong imagination.

Moved by some impulse which she could not have explained, the Baroness left her guest and made her way to the narrow, cheerless room where the old governess lay watching the hours of the dying year slip by. In spite of the biting cold of the winter night, the window stood open. With a scandalized exclamation on her lips, the Baroness rushed forward to close it.

"Leave it open," said the old woman in a voice that for all its weakness carried an air of command such as the Baroness had never heard before from her lips.

"But you will die of cold!" she expostulated.

"I am dying in any case," said the voice, "and I want to hear their music. They have come from far and wide to sing the death music of my family. It is beautiful that they have come; I am the last von Cernogratz that will die in our old castle, and they have come to sing to me. Hark, how loud they are calling!"

The cry of the wolves rose on the still winter air and floated round the castle walls in long-drawn piercing wails; the old woman lay back on her couch with a look of long-delayed happiness on her face.

"Go away," she said to the Baroness; "I am not lonely any more. I am one of a great old family. . . ."

"I think she is dying," said the Baroness when she had rejoined her guests; "I suppose we must send for a doctor. And that terrible howling! Not for much money would I have such death music."

"That music is not to be bought for any amount of money," said Conrad.

"Hark! What is that other sound?" asked the Baron, as a noise of splitting and crashing was heard.

It was a tree falling in the park.

There was a moment of constrained silence, and then the banker's wife spoke.

"It is the intense cold that is splitting the trees. It is also the cold that has brought the wolves out in

such numbers. It is many years since we have
had such a cold winter."

The Baroness eagerly agreed that the cold was responsible for these things. It was the cold of the
open window, too, which caused the heart failure
that made the doctor's ministrations unnecessary for
the old Fraulein. But the notice in the newspapers
looked very well:

On December 29th, at Schloss Cernogratz, Amalie von Cernogratz, for many years the valued friend
of Baron and Baroness Gruebel.

The Guests

"THE landscape seen from our windows is certainly charming," said Annabel; "those cherry orchards and green meadows, and the river winding along the valley, and the church tower peeping out among the elms, they all make a most effective picture. There's something dreadfully sleepy and languorous about it, though; stagnation seems to be the dominant note. Nothing ever happens here; seedtime and harvest, an occasional outbreak of measles or a mildly destructive thunderstorm, and a little election excitement about once in five years, that is all that we have to modify the monotony of our existence. Rather dreadful, isn't it?"

"On the contrary," said Matilda, "I find it soothing and restful; but then, you see, I've lived in countries where things do happen, ever so many at a time, when you're not ready for them happening all at once."

"That, of course, makes a difference," said Annabel.

"I have never forgotten," said Matilda, "the occasion when the Bishop of Bequar paid us an unexpected visit; he was on his way to lay the foundation stone of a mission house or something of the sort."

"I thought that out there you were always prepared for emergency guests turning up," said Annabel.

"I was quite prepared for half a dozen bishops," said Matilda, "but it was rather disconcerting to find out after a little conversation that this particular one was a distant cousin of mine, belonging to a branch of the family that had quarrelled bitterly and offensively with our branch about a Crown Derby dessert service; they got it, and we ought to have got it, in some legacy, or else we got it and they thought they ought to have it, I forget which; anyhow, I know they behaved disgracefully. Now here was one of them turning up in the odour of sanctity, so to speak, and claiming the traditional hospitality of the East."

"It was rather trying, but you could have left your husband to do most of the entertaining."

"My husband was fifty miles upcountry, talking sense, or what he imagined to be sense, to a village community that fancied one of their leading men was a weretiger."

"A what tiger?"

"A weretiger; you've heard of werewolves, haven't you, a mixture of wolf and human being and demon? Well, in those parts they have weretigers, or think they have, and I must say that in this case, so far as sworn and uncontested evidence went, they had every ground for thinking so. However, as we gave up witchcraft prosecutions about three hundred years ago, we don't like to have other people keeping on our discarded practises; it doesn't seem respectful to our mental and moral position."

"I hope you weren't unkind to the Bishop," said Annabel.

"Well, of course he was my guest, so I had to be outwardly polite to him, but he was tactless enough to rake up the incidents of the old quarrel, and to try to make out that there was something to be said for the way his side of the family had behaved; even if there was, which I don't for a moment admit, my house was not the place in which to say it. I didn't argue the matter, but I gave my cook a holiday to go and visit his aged parents some ninety miles away. The emergency cook was not a specialist in curries; in fact, I don't think cooking in any shape or form could have been one of his strong points. I believe he originally came to us in the guise of a gardener, but as we never pretended to have anything that could be considered a garden he was utilized as assistant goatherd, in which capacity, I understand, he gave every satisfaction. When the Bishop heard that I had sent away the cook on a special and unnecessary holiday, he saw the inwardness of the manoeuvre, and from that moment we were scarcely on speaking terms. If you have ever had a Bishop with whom you were not on speaking terms staying in your house, you will appreciate the situation."

Annabel confessed that her life story had never included such a disturbing experience.

"Then," continued Matilda, "to make matters more complicated, the Gwadlipichee overflowed its banks, a thing it did every now and then when the rains were unduly prolonged, and the lower part of the house and all the outbuildings were submerged. We managed to get the ponies loose in time, and the syce swam the whole lot of them off to the nearest rising ground. A goat or two, the chief goatherd, the chief goatherd's wife, and several of their babies came to anchorage in the verandah. All the rest of the available space was filled up with wet, bedraggled-looking hens and chickens; one never really knows how many fowls one possesses till the servants' quarters are flooded out. Of course, I had been through something of the sort in previous floods, but never before had I had a houseful of goats and babies and half-drowned hens, supplemented by a bishop with whom I was hardly on speaking terms."

"It must have been a trying experience," commented Annabel.

"More embarrassments were to follow. I wasn't going to let a mere ordinary flood wash out the memory of that Crown Derby dessert service, and I intimated to the Bishop that his large bedroom, with a writing table in it, and his small bathroom, with a sufficiency of cold-water jars in it, was his share of the premises, and that space was rather congested under the existing circumstances. However, at about three o'clock in the afternoon, when he had awakened from his midday sleep, he made a sudden incursion into the room that was normally the drawing room, but was now dining room, storehouse, saddle room, and half a dozen other temporary premises as well. From the condition of my guest's costume he seemed to think it might also serve as his dressing room.

" 'I'm afraid there is nowhere for you to sit,' I said coldly; 'the verandah is full of goats.'

" 'There is a goat in my bedroom,' he observed with equal coldness, and more than a suspicion of sardonic reproach.

" 'Really,' I said, 'another survivor! I thought all the other goats were done for.'

" 'This particular goat is quite done for,' he said; 'it is being devoured by a leopard at the present moment. That is why I left the room; some animals resent being watched while they are eating.'

"The leopard, of course, was easily explained; it had been hanging round the goat sheds when the flood came, and had clambered up by the outside staircase leading to the Bishop's bathroom, thoughtfully bringing a goat with it. Probably it found the bathroom too damp and shut-in for its taste, and transferred its banqueting operations to the bedroom while the Bishop was having his nap."

"What a frightful situation!" exclaimed Annabel; "fancy having a ravening leopard in the house, with a flood all round you."

"Not in the least ravening," said Matilda; "it was full of goat, had any amount of water at its disposal if it felt thirsty, and probably had no more immediate wish than a desire for uninterrupted sleep. Still, I think anyone will admit that it was an embarrassing predicament to have your only available guest room occupied by a leopard, the verandah choked up with goats and babies and wet hens, and a bishop with whom you were scarcely on speaking terms planted down in your only sitting room. I really don't know how I got through those crawling hours, and of course mealtimes only made matters worse. The emergency cook had every excuse for sending in watery soup and sloppy rice, and as neither the chief goatherd nor his wife were expert divers, the cellar could not be reached. Fortunately the Gwadlipichee subsides as rapidly as it rises, and just before dawn the syce came splashing back, with the ponies only fetlock deep in water. Then there arose some awkwardness from the fact that the Bishop wished to leave sooner than the leopard did, and as the latter was ensconced in the midst of the former's personal possessions there was an obvious difficulty in altering the order of departure. I pointed out to the Bishop that a leopard's habits and tastes are not those of an otter, and that it naturally preferred walking to wading, and that in any case a meal of an entire goat, washed down with tub water, justified a certain amount of repose; if I had had guns fired to frighten the animal away, as the Bishop suggested, it would probably merely have left the bedroom to come into the already overcrowded drawing room. Altogether it was rather a relief when they both left. Now, perhaps, you can understand my appreciation of a sleepy countryside where things don't happen."

The Penance

OCTAVIAN RUTTLE was one of those lively, cheerful
individuals on whom amiability had set its un-
mistakable stamp, and, like most of their kind, his
soul's peace depended in large measure on the unstinted approval of his fellows. In hunting to death a
small tabby cat he had done a thing of which he
scarcely approved himself, and he was glad when
the gardener had hidden the body in its hastily dug
grave under a lonely oak tree in the meadow, the
same tree that the hunted quarry had climbed as a
last effort towards safety. It had been a distasteful
and seemingly ruthless deed, but circumstances had
demanded the doing of it. Octavian kept chickens; at
least he kept some of them; others vanished from his
keeping, leaving only a few bloodstained feathers to
mark the manner of their going. The tabby cat from
the large grey house that stood with its back to the
meadow had been detected in many furtive visits to
the hen coops, and after due negotiation with those
in authority at the grey house a sentence of death had
been agreed on: "The children will mind, but they
need not know," had been the last word on the matter.

The children in question were a standing puzzle to
Octavian; in the course of a few months he con-

sidered that he should have known their names, ages, the dates of their birthdays, and have been introduced to their favourite toys. They remained, however, as noncommittal as the long blank wall that shut them off from the meadow, a wall over which their three heads sometimes appeared at odd moments. They had parents in India—that much Octavian had learned in the neighbourhood; the children, beyond grouping themselves garmentwise into sexes, a girl and two boys, carried their life story no further on his behoof. And now it seemed he was engaged in something which touched them closely, but must be hidden from their knowledge.

The poor helpless chickens had gone one by one to their doom, so it was meet that their destroyer should come to a violent end, yet Octavian felt some qualms when his share of the violence was ended. The little cat, headed off from its wonted tracks of safety, had raced unfriended from shelter to shelter, and its end had been rather piteous. Octavian walked through the long grass of the meadow with a step less jaunty than usual. And as he passed beneath the shadow of the high blank wall he glanced up and became aware that his hunting had had undesired witnesses. Three white faces were looking down at him, and if ever an artist wanted a threefold study of cold human hate, impotent yet unyielding, raging yet masked in stillness, he would have found it in the triple gaze that met Octavian's eye.

"I'm sorry, but it had to be done," said Octavian, with genuine apology in his voice.

"Beast!"

The answer came from three throats with startling intensity.

Octavian felt that the blank wall would not be more impervious to his explanations than the bunch of human hostility that peered over its coping; he wisely decided to withhold his peace overtures till a more hopeful occasion.

Two days later he ransacked the best sweetshop in the neighbouring market town for a box of chocolates that by its size and contents should fitly atone for the dismal deed done under the oak tree in the meadow. The first two specimens that were shown to him he hastily rejected; one had a group of chickens pictured on its lid, the other bore the portrait of a tabby kitten. A third sample was more simply bedecked with a spray of painted poppies, and Octavian hailed the flowers of forgetfulness as a happy omen. He felt distinctly more at ease with his surroundings when the imposing package had been sent across to the grey house, and a message returned to say that it had been duly given to the children. The next morning he sauntered with purposeful steps past the long blank wall on his way to the chicken run and piggery that stood at the bottom of the meadow. The three children were perched at their accustomed lookout, and their range of sight did not seem to concern itself with Octavian's presence. As he became depressingly aware of the aloofness of their gaze he also noted a strange variegation in the herbage at his feet; the greensward for a considerable space around was strewn and speckled with a chocolate-coloured hail, enlivened here and there with gay tinsellike wrappings or the glistening mauve of crystallized violets. It was as though the fairy paradise of a greedy-minded child had taken shape and substance in the vegetation of the meadow. Octavian's blood money had been flung back at him in scorn.

To increase his discomfiture the march of events tended to shift the blame of ravaged chicken coops from the supposed culprit who had already paid full forfeit; the young chicks were still carried off, and it seemed highly probable that the cat had only haunted the chicken run to prey on the rats which harboured there. Through the flowing channels of servant talk the children learned of this belated revision of verdict, and Octavian one day picked up a sheet of copybook paper on which was painstakingly written: "Beast. Rats eated your chickens." More ardently than ever did he wish for an opportunity for sloughing off the disgrace that enwrapped him, and earning some happier nickname from his three unsparing judges.

And one day a chance inspiration came to him. Olivia, his two-year-old daughter, was accustomed to spend the hour from high noon till one o'clock with her father while the nursemaid gobbled and digested her dinner and novelette. About the same time the blank wall was usually enlivened by the presence of its three small wardens. Octavian, with seeming carelessness of purpose, brought Olivia well within hail of the watchers and noted with hidden delight the growing interest that dawned in that hitherto sternly hostile quarter. His little Olivia, with her sleepy placid ways, was going to succeed where he, with his anxious well-meant overtures, had so signally failed. He brought her a large yellow dahlia, which she grasped tightly in one hand and regarded with a stare of benevolent boredom, such as one might bestow on amateur classical dancing performed in aid of a deserving charity. Then he turned shyly to the group perched on the wall and asked with affected carelessness, "Do you like flowers?" Three solemn nods rewarded his venture.

"Which sorts do you like best?" he asked, this time with a distinct betrayal of eagerness in his voice.

"Those with all the colours, over there." Three chubby arms pointed to a distant tangle of sweet pea. Childlike, they had asked for what lay farthest from hand, but Octavian trotted off gleefully to obey their welcome behest. He pulled and plucked with unsparing hand, and brought every variety of tint that he could see into his bunch that was rapidly becoming a bundle. Then he turned to retrace his steps, and found the blank wall blanker and more deserted than ever, while the foreground was void of all trace of Olivia. Far down the meadow three children were pushing a go-cart at the utmost speed they could muster in the direction of the piggeries; it was Olivia's go-cart and Olivia sat in it, somewhat bumped and shaken by the pace at which she was being driven but apparently retaining her wonted composure of mind. Octavian stared for a moment at the rapidly moving group, and then started in hot pursuit, shedding, as he ran, sprays of blossom from the mass of sweet pea that he still clutched in his hands. Fast as he ran, the children had reached the piggery before he could overtake them, and he arrived just in time to see Olivia, wondering but unprotesting, hauled and pushed up to the roof of the nearest sty. They were old buildings in some need of repair, and the rickety roof would certainly not have borne Octavian's weight if he had attempted to follow his daughter and her captors to their new vantage ground.

"What are you going to do with her?" he panted.

There was no mistaking the grim trend of mischief in those flushed but sternly composed young faces.

"Hang her in chains over a slow fire," said one of the boys. Evidently they had been reading English history.

"Frow her down and the pigs will d'vour her, every bit 'cept the palms of her hands," said the other boy. It was also evident that they had studied Biblical history.

The last proposal was the one which most alarmed Octavian, since it might be carried into effect at a moment's notice; there had been cases, he remembered, of pigs eating babies.

"You surely wouldn't treat my poor little Olivia in that way?" he pleaded.

"You killed our little cat," came in stern reminder from three throats.

"I'm very sorry I did," said Octavian, and if there is a standard of measurement in truths Octavian's statement was assuredly a large nine.

"We shall be very sorry when we've killed Olivia," said the girl, "but we can't be sorry till we've done it."

The inexorable child logic rose like an unyielding rampart before Octavian's scared pleadings. Before he could think of any fresh line of appeal his energies were called out in another direction. Olivia had slid off the roof and fallen with a soft, unctuous splash into a morass of muck and decaying straw. Octavian scrambled hastily over the pigsty wall to her rescue, and at once found himself in a quagmire that engulfed his feet. Olivia, after the first shock of surprise at her sudden drop through the air, had been mildly pleased at finding herself in close and unstinted contact with the sticky element that oozed around her, but as she began to sink gently into the bed of slime, a feeling dawned on her that she was not after all very happy, and she began to cry in the tentative fashion of the normally good child. Octavian, battling with the quagmire, which seemed to have learned the rare art of giving way at all points without yielding an inch, saw his daughter slowly disappearing in the engulfing slush, her smeared face further distorted with the contortions of whimpering wonder, while from their perch on the pigsty roof the three children looked down with the cold unpitying detachment of the Parcae Sisters.

"I can't reach her in time," gasped Octavian; "she'll be choked in the muck. Won't you help her?"

"No one helped our cat," came the inevitable reminder.

"I'll do anything to show you how sorry I am about that," cried Octavian, with a further desperate flounder, which carried him scarcely two inches forward.

"Will you stand in a white sheet by the grave?"

"Yes," screamed Octavian.

"Holding a candle?"

"An' saying, 'I'm a miserable Beast'?"

Octavian agreed to both suggestions.

"For a long, long time?"

"For half an hour," said Octavian. There was an anxious ring in his voice as he named the time limit; was there not the precedent of a German king who did open-air penance for several days and nights at Christmas time clad only in his shirt? Fortunately the children did not appear to have read German history, and half an hour seemed long and goodly in their eyes.

"All right," came with threefold solemnity from the

roof, and a moment later a short ladder had been laboriously pushed across to Octavian, who lost no time in propping it against the low pigsty wall. Scrambling gingerly along its rungs he was able to lean across the morass that separated him from his slowly foundering offspring and extract her like an unwilling cork from its slushy embrace. A few minutes later he was listening to the shrill and repeated assurances of the nursemaid that her previous experience of filthy spectacles had been on a notably smaller scale.

That same evening when twilight was deepening into darkness Octavian took up his position as penitent under the lone oak tree, having first carefully undressed the part. Clad in a zephyr shirt, which on this occasion thoroughly merited its name, he held in one hand a lighted candle and in the other a watch, into which the soul of a dead plumber seemed to have passed. A box of matches lay at his feet and was resorted to on the fairly frequent occasions when the candle succumbed to the night breezes. The house loomed inscrutable in the middle distance, but as Octavian conscientiously repeated the formula of his penance he felt certain that three pairs of solemn eyes were watching his moth-shared vigil.

And the next morning his eyes were gladdened by a sheet of copybook paper lying beside the blank wall, on which was written the message "un-Beast."

The Interlopers

IN A forest of mixed growth somewhere on the east-
ern spurs of the Carpathians, a man stood one
winter night, watching and listening, as though he
waited for some beast of the woods to come within
the range of his vision, and later of his rifle. But the
game for whose presence he kept so keen an outlook
was none that figured in the sportsman's calendar as
lawful and proper for the chase; Ulrich von Gradwitz
patrolled the dark forest in quest of a human enemy.

The forest lands of Gradwitz were of wide extent
and well stocked with game; the narrow strip of
precipitous woodland that lay on its outskirt was not
remarkable for the game it harboured or the shooting
it afforded, but it was the most jealously guarded of
all its owner's territorial possessions. A famous law-
suit, in the days of his grandfather, had wrested it
from the illegal possession of a neighbouring family
of petty landowners; the dispossessed party had
never acquiesced in the judgment of the courts, and
a long series of poaching affrays and similar scandals
had embittered the relationships between the families
for three generations. The neighbour feud had grown
into a personal one since Ulrich had come to be head
of his family; if there was a man in the world whom
he detested and wished ill to it was Georg Znaeym,

the inheritor of the quarrel and the tireless game snatcher and raider of the disputed border forest. The feud might, perhaps, have died down or been compromised if the personal ill will of the two men had not stood in the way; as boys they had thirsted for one another's blood; as men each prayed that misfortune might fall on the other, and this wind-scourged winter night Ulrich had banded together his foresters to watch the dark forest, not in quest of four-footed quarry, but to keep a lookout for the prowling thieves whom he suspected of being afoot from across the land boundary. The roebuck, which usually kept in the sheltered hollows during a storm wind, were running like driven things tonight, and there was movement and unrest among the creatures that were wont to sleep through the dark hours. Assuredly there was a disturbing element in the forest, and Ulrich could guess the quarter from whence it came.

He strayed away by himself from the watchers whom he had placed in ambush on the crest of the hill, and wandered far down the steep slopes amid the wild tangle of undergrowth, peering through the tree trunks and listening through the whistling and skirling of the wind and the restless beating of the branches for sight or sound of the marauders. If only on this wild night, in this dark, lone spot, he might come across Georg Znaeym, man to man, with none to witness—that was the wish that was uppermost in his thoughts. And as he stepped round the trunk of a huge beech he came face to face with the man he sought.

The two enemies stood glaring at one another for a long silent moment. Each had a rifle in his hand, each had hate in his heart and murder uppermost in

his mind. The chance had come to give full play to
the passions of a lifetime. But a man who has been
brought up under the code of a restraining civiliza-
tion cannot easily nerve himself to shoot down his
neighbour in cold blood without a word spoken,
except for an offence against his hearth and honour.
And before the moment of hesitation had given way
to action, a deed of Nature's own violence over-
whelmed them both. A fierce shriek of the storm had
been answered by a splitting crash over their heads,
and ere they could leap aside, a mass of falling
beech tree had thundered down on them. Ulrich von
Gradwitz found himself stretched on the ground, one
arm numb beneath him and the other held almost as
helplessly in a tight tangle of forked branches, while
both legs were pinned beneath the fallen mass. His
heavy shooting boots had saved his feet from being
crushed to pieces, but if his fractures were not as serious as they might have been, at least it was evident
that he could not move from his present position till
someone came to release him. The descending twigs
had slashed the skin of his face, and he had to wink
away some drops of blood from his eyelashes before
he could take in a general view of the disaster. At his
side, so near that under ordinary circumstances he
could almost have touched him, lay Georg Znaeym,
alive and struggling, but obviously as helplessly pin-
ioned down as himself. All around them lay a thick-
strewn wreckage of splintered branches and broken
twigs.

Relief at being alive and exasperation at his captive
plight brought a strange medley of pious thank offer-
ings and sharp curses to Ulrich's lips. Georg, who was
nearly blinded with the blood which trickled across

his eyes, stopped his struggling for a moment to listen, and then gave a short, snarling laugh.

"So you're not killed, as you ought to be, but you're caught, anyway," he cried; "caught fast. Ho, what a jest, Ulrich von Gradwitz snared in his stolen forest. There's real justice for you!"

And he laughed again, mockingly and savagely.

"I'm caught in my own forest land," retorted Ulrich. "When my men come to release us you will wish, perhaps, that you were in a better plight than caught poaching on a neighbour's land, shame on you."

Georg was silent for a moment; then he answered quietly:

"Are you sure that your men will find much to release? I have men, too, in the forest tonight, close behind me, and *they* will be here first and do the releasing. When they drag me out from under these branches it won't need much clumsiness on their part to roll this mass of trunk right over on top of you. Your men will find you dead under a fallen beech tree. For form's sake I shall send my condolences to your family."

"It is a useful hint," said Ulrich fiercely. "My men had orders to follow in ten minutes' time, seven of which must have gone by already, and when they get me out—I will remember the hint. Only as you will have met your death poaching on my lands I don't think I can decently send any message of condolence to your family."

"Good," snarled Georg, "good. We fight this quarrel out to the death, you and I and our foresters, with no cursed interlopers to come between us. Death and damnation to you, Ulrich von Gradwitz."

"The same to you, Georg Znaeym, forest thief, game snatcher."

Both men spoke with the bitterness of possible defeat before them, for each knew that it might be long before his men would seek him out or find him; it was a bare matter of chance which party would arrive first on the scene.

Both had now given up the useless struggle to free themselves from the mass of wood that held them down; Ulrich limited his endeavours to an effort to bring his one partially free arm near enough to his outer coat pocket to draw out his wine flask. Even when he had accomplished that operation it was long before he could manage the unscrewing of the stopper or get any of the liquid down his throat. But what a Heaven-sent draught it seemed! It was an open winter, and little snow had fallen as yet, hence the captives suffered less from the cold than might have been the case at that season of the year; nevertheless, the wine was warming and reviving to the wounded man, and he looked across with something like a throb of pity to where his enemy lay, just keeping the groans of pain and weariness from crossing his lips.

"Could you reach this flask if I threw it over to you?" asked Ulrich suddenly; "there is good wine in it, and one may as well be as comfortable as one can. Let us drink, even if tonight one of us dies."

"No, I can scarcely see anything; there is so much blood caked round my eyes," said Georg, "and in any case I don't drink wine with an enemy."

Ulrich was silent for a few minutes, and lay listening to the weary screeching of the wind. An idea was slowly forming and growing in his brain, an idea that gained strength every time that he looked across at the man who was fighting so grimly against pain and exhaustion. In the pain and languor that Ulrich himself was feeling, the old fierce hatred seemed to be dying down.

"Neighbour," he said presently, "do as you please if your men come first. It was a fair compact. But as for me, I've changed my mind. If my men are the first to come you shall be the first to be helped, as though you were my guest. We have quarrelled like devils all our lives over this stupid strip of forest, where the trees can't even stand upright in a breath of wind. Lying here tonight, thinking, I've come to think we've been rather fools; there are better things in life than getting the better of a boundary dispute. Neighbour, if you will help me to bury the old quarrel I—I will ask you to be my friend."

Georg Znaeym was silent for so long that Ulrich thought, perhaps, he had fainted with the pain of his injuries. Then he spoke slowly and in jerks.

"How the whole region would stare and gabble if we rode into the market square together. No one living can remember seeing a Znaeym and a von Gradwitz talking to one another in friendship. And what peace there would be among the forester folk if we ended our feud tonight. And if we choose to make peace among our people there is none other to interfere, no interlopers from outside. . . . You would come and keep the Sylvester night beneath my roof, and I would come and feast on some high day at your castle. . . . I would never fire a shot on your land, save when you invited me as a guest; and you should come and shoot with me down in the marshes where the wildfowl are. In all the countryside there are none that could hinder if we willed to make peace. I never thought to have wanted to do other than hate you all my life, but I think I have changed my mind about things too, this last half hour. And you offered me your wine flask. . . . Ulrich von Gradwitz, I will be your friend."

For a space both men were silent, turning over in their minds the wonderful changes that this dramatic reconciliation would bring about. In the cold, gloomy forest, with the wind tearing in fitful gusts through the naked branches and whistling round the tree trunks, they lay and waited for the help that would now bring release and succour to both parties. And each prayed a private prayer that his men might be the first to arrive, so that he might be the first to show honourable attention to the enemy that had become a friend.

Presently, as the wind dropped for a moment, Ulrich broke the silence.

"Let's shout for help," he said; "in this lull our voices may carry a little way."

"They won't carry far through the trees and undergrowth," said Georg, "but we can try. Together, then."

The two raised their voices in a prolonged hunting call.

"Together again," said Ulrich a few minutes later, after listening in vain for an answering halloo.

"I heard something that time, I think," said Ulrich.

"I heard nothing but the pestilential wind," said Georg hoarsely.

There was silence again for some minutes, and then Ulrich gave a joyful cry.

"I can see figures coming through the wood. They

are following in the way I came down the hillside."

Both men raised their voices in as loud a shout as they could muster.

"They hear us! They've stopped. Now they see us. They're running down the hill towards us," cried Ulrich.

"How many of them are there?" asked Georg.

"I can't see distinctly," said Ulrich; "nine or ten."

"Then they are yours," said Georg; "I had only seven out with me."

"They are making all the speed they can, brave lads," said Ulrich gladly.

"Are they your men?" asked Georg. "Are they your men?" he repeated impatiently as Ulrich did not answer.

"No," said Ulrich with a laugh, the idiotic chattering laugh of a man unstrung with hideous fear.

"Who are they?" asked Georg quickly, straining his eyes to see what the other would gladly not have seen.

"*Wolves.*"

The Mappined Life

"THESE Mappin Terraces at the Zoological Gardens are a great improvement on the old style of wild-beast cage," said Mrs. James Gurtleberry, putting down an illustrated paper; "they give one the illusion of seeing the animals in their natural surroundings. I wonder how much of the illusion is passed on to the animals?"

"That would depend on the animal," said her niece; "a jungle fowl, for instance, would no doubt think its lawful jungle surroundings were faithfully reproduced if you gave it a sufficiency of wives, a goodly variety of seed food and ants' eggs, a commodious bank of loose earth to dust itself in, a convenient roosting tree, and a rival or two to make matters interesting. Of course, there ought to be jungle cats and birds of prey and other agencies of sudden death to add to the illusion of liberty, but the bird's own imagination is capable of inventing those—look how a domestic fowl will squawk an alarm note if a rook or wood pigeon passes over its run when it has chickens."

"You think, then, they really do have a sort of illusion, if you give them space enough——"

"In a few cases only. Nothing will make me believe that an acre or so of concrete enclosure will make up to a wolf or a tiger cat for the range of night prowling that would belong to it in a wild state. Think of the dictionary of sound and scent and recollection that unfolds before a real wild beast as it comes out from its lair every evening, with the knowledge that in a few minutes it will be hieing along to some distant hunting ground where all the joy and fury of the chase awaits it; think of the crowded sensations of the brain when every rustle, every cry, every bent twig, and every whiff across the nostrils means something, something to do with life and death and dinner. Imagine the satisfaction of stealing down to your own particular drinking spot, choosing your own particular tree to scrape your claws on, finding your own particular bed of dried grass to roll on. Then, in the place of all that, put a concrete promenade, which will be of exactly the same dimensions whether you race or crawl across it, coated with stale, unvarying scents and surrounded with cries and noises that have ceased to have the least meaning or interest. As a substitute for a narrow cage the new enclosures are excellent, but I should think they are a poor imitation of a life of liberty."

"It's rather depressing to think that," said Mrs. Gurtleberry; "they look so spacious and so natural, but I suppose a good deal of what seems natural to us would be meaningless to a wild animal."

"That is where our superior powers of self-deception come in," said the niece; "we are able to live our unreal, stupid little lives on our particular Mappin Terrace, and persuade ourselves that we really are untrammelled men and women leading a reasonable existence in a reasonable sphere."

"But good gracious," exclaimed the aunt, bouncing into an attitude of scandalized defence, "we are leading reasonable existences! What on earth do you mean by trammels? We are merely trammelled by the ordinary decent conventions of civilized society."

"We are trammelled," said the niece, calmly and pitilessly, "by restrictions of income and opportunity, and above all by lack of initiative. To some people a restricted income doesn't matter a bit, in fact it often seems to help as a means for getting a lot of reality out of life; I am sure there are men and women who do their shopping in little back streets of Paris, buying four carrots and a shred of beef for their daily sustenance, who lead a perfectly real and eventful existence. Lack of initiative is the thing that really cripples one, and that is where you and I and Uncle James are so hopelessly shut in. We are just so many animals stuck down on a Mappin Terrace, to be looked at, while nobody wants to look at us. As a matter of fact there would be nothing to look at. We get colds in winter and hay fever in summer, and if a wasp happens to sting one of us, well, that is the wasp's initiative, not ours; all we do is to wait for the swelling to go down. Whenever we do climb into local fame and notice, it is by indirect methods; if it happens to be a good flowering year for magnolias the neighbourhood observes, 'Have you seen the Gurtleberrys' magnolia? It is a perfect mass of flowers,' and we go about telling people that there are fifty-seven blossoms as against thirty-nine the previous year."

"In Coronation year there were as many as sixty," put in the aunt; "your uncle has kept a record for the last eight years."

"Doesn't it ever strike you," continued the niece

relentlessly, "that if we moved away from here or were blotted out of existence our local claim to fame would pass on automatically to whoever happened to take the house and garden? People would say to one another, 'Have you seen the Smith-Jenkins' magnolia? It is a perfect mass of flowers,' or else, 'Smith-Jenkins tells me there won't be a single blossom on their magnolia this year; the east winds have turned all the buds black.' Now if, when we had gone, people still associated our names with the magnolia tree, no matter who temporarily possessed it, if they said, 'Ah, that's the tree on which the Gurtleberrys hung their cook because she sent up the wrong kind of sauce with the asparagus,' that would be something really due to our own initiative, apart from anything east winds of magnolia vitality might have to say in the matter."

"We should never do such a thing," said the aunt. The niece gave a reluctant sigh.

"I can't imagine it," she admitted. "Of course," she continued, "there are heaps of ways of leading a real existence without committing sensational deeds of violence. It's the dreadful little everyday acts of pretended importance that give the Mappin stamp to our life. It would be entertaining, if it weren't so pathetically tragic, to hear Uncle James fuss in here in the morning and announce, 'I must just go down into the town and find out what the men there are saying about Mexico. Matters are beginning to look serious there.' Then he patters away into the town, and talks in a highly serious voice to the tobacconist, incidentally buying an ounce of tobacco; perhaps he meets one or two others of the world's thinkers and talks to them in a highly serious voice, then he patters back here and announces with increased importance, 'I've just been talking to some men in the town about the condition of affairs in Mexico. They agree with the view that I have formed, that things there will have to get worse before they get better.' Of course nobody in the town cared in the least little bit what his views about Mexico were or whether he had any. The tobacconist wasn't even flattered at his buying the ounce of tobacco; he knows that he purchases the same quantity of the same sort of tobacco every week. Uncle James might just as well have lain on his back in the garden and chattered to the lilac tree about the habits of caterpillars."

"I really will not listen to such things about your uncle," protested Mrs. James Gurtleberry angrily.

"My own case is just as bad and just as tragic," said the niece dispassionately; "nearly everything about me is conventional make-believe. I'm not a good dancer, and no one could honestly call me good-looking, but when I go to one of our dull little local dances I'm conventionally supposed to 'have a heavenly time,' to attract the ardent homage of the local cavaliers, and to go home with my head awhirl with pleasurable recollections. As a matter of fact, I've merely put in some hours of indifferent dancing, drunk some badly made claret cup, and listened to an enormous amount of laborious light conversation. A moonlight hen-stealing raid with the merry-eyed curate would be infinitely more exciting; imagine the pleasure of carrying off all those white Minorcas that the Chibfords are always bragging about. When we had disposed of them we could give the proceeds to a charity, so there would be nothing really wrong about it. But nothing of that sort lies within the Mappined limits of my life. One of these days somebody dull and decorous and undistinguished will 'make himself agreeable' to me at a tennis party, as the saying is, and all the dull old gossips of the neighbourhood will begin to ask when we are to be engaged, and at last we shall be engaged, and people will give us butter dishes and blotting cases and framed pictures of young women feeding swans. Hullo, Uncle, are you going out?"

"I'm just going down to the town," announced Mr. James Gurtleberry, with an air of some importance: "I want to hear what people are saying about Albania. Affairs there are beginning to take on a very serious look. It's my opinion that we haven't seen the worst of things yet."

In this he was probably right, but there was nothing in the immediate or prospective condition of Albania to warrant Mrs. Gurtleberry in bursting into tears.

The Seven Cream Jugs

"**I** SUPPOSE we shall never see Wilfrid Pigeoncote
here now that he has become heir to the baronetcy and to a lot of money," observed Mrs. Peter
Pigeoncote regretfully to her husband.

"Well, we can hardly expect to," he replied, "seeing that we always choked him off from coming to
see us when he was a prospective nobody. I don't
think I've set eyes on him since he was a boy of
twelve."

"There was a reason for not wanting to encourage
his acquaintanceship," said Mrs. Peter. "With the notorious failing of his he was not the sort of person
one wanted in one's house."

"Well, the failing still exists, doesn't it?" said her
husband; "or do you suppose a reform of character
is entailed along with the estate?"

"Oh, of course, there is still that drawback," admitted the wife, "but one would like to make the
acquaintance of the future head of the family, if only
out of mere curiosity. Besides, cynicism apart, his
being rich *will* make a difference in the way people
will look at his failing. When a man is absolutely
wealthy, not merely well to do, all suspicion of sordid
motive naturally disappears; the thing becomes merely a tiresome malady."

Wilfrid Pigeoncote had suddenly become heir to his uncle, Sir Wilfrid Pigeoncote, on the death of his cousin, Major Wilfrid Pigeoncote, who had succumbed to the aftereffects of a polo accident. (A Wilfrid Pigeoncote had covered himself with honours in the course of Marlborough's campaigns, and the name Wilfrid had been a baptismal weakness in the family ever since.) The new heir to the family dignity and estates was a young man of about five-and-twenty, who was known more by reputation than by person to a wide circle of cousins and kinsfolk. And the reputation was an unpleasant one. The numerous other Wilfrids in the family were distinguished one from another chiefly by the names of their residences or professions, as Wilfrid of Hubbledown, and young Wilfrid the Gunner, but this particular scion was known by the ignominious and expressive label of Wilfrid the Snatcher. From his late school days onward he had been possessed by an acute and obstinate form of kleptomania: he had the acquisitive instinct of the collector without any of the collector's discrimination. Anything that was smaller and more portable than a sideboard and above the value of ninepence had an irresistible attraction for him, provided that it fulfilled the necessary condition of belonging to someone else. On the rare occasions when he was included in a country-house party, it was usual and almost necessary for his host, or some member of the family, to make a friendly inquisition through his baggage on the eve of his departure, to see if he had packed up "by mistake" anyone else's property. The search usually produced a large and varied yield.

"This is funny," said Peter Pigeoncote to his wife,

some half-hour after their conversation; "here's a telegram from Wilfrid, saying he's passing through here in his motor, and would like to stop and pay us his respects. Can stay for the night if it doesn't inconvenience us. Signed 'Wilfrid Pigeoncote.' Must be the Snatcher; none of the others have a motor. I suppose he's bringing us a present for the silver wedding."

"Good gracious!" said Mrs. Peter, as a thought struck her; "this is rather an awkward time to have a person with his failing in the house. All those silver presents set out in the drawing room, and others coming by every post; I hardly know what we've got and what are still to come. We can't lock them all up; he's sure to want to see them."

"We must keep a sharp lookout, that's all," said Peter reassuringly.

"But these practised kleptomaniacs are so clever," said his wife apprehensively, "and it will be so awkward if he suspects that we are watching him."

Awkwardness was indeed the prevailing note that evening when the passing traveller was being entertained. The talk flitted nervously and hurriedly from one impersonal topic to another. The guest had none of the furtive, half-apologetic air that his cousins had rather expected to find; his was polite, well-assured, and, perhaps, just a little inclined to "put on side." His hosts, on the other hand, wore an uneasy manner that might have been the hallmark of conscious depravity. In the drawing room, after dinner, their nervousness and awkwardness increased.

"Oh, we haven't shown you the silver-wedding presents," said Mrs. Peter suddenly, as though struck by a brilliant idea for entertaining the guest; "here

they all are. Such nice, useful gifts. A few duplicates, of course."

"Seven cream jugs," put in Peter.

"Yes, isn't it annoying," went on Mrs. Peter; "seven
of them. We feel that we must live on cream for the
rest of our lives. Of course, some of them can be
changed."

Wilfrid occupied himself chiefly with such of the
gifts as were of antique interest, carrying one or
two of them over to the lamp to examine their marks.
The anxiety of his hosts at these moments re-
sembled the solicitude of a cat whose newly born
kittens are being handed round for inspection.

"Let me see; did you give me back the mustard
pot? This is its place here," piped Mrs. Peter.

"Sorry. I put it down by the claret jug," said
Wilfrid, busy with another object.

"Oh, just let me have that sugar sifter again,"
asked Mrs. Peter, dogged determination showing
through her nervousness. "I must label it who it
comes from before I forget."

Vigilance was not completely crowned with a sense
of victory. After they had said "Good night" to their
visitor, Mrs. Peter expressed her conviction that he
had taken something.

"I fancy, by his manner, that there was something
up," corroborated her husband. "Do you miss anything?"

Mrs. Peter hastily counted the array of gifts.

"I can only make it thirty-four, and I think it should
be thirty-five," she announced. "I can't remember if
thirty-five includes the Archdeacon's cruet stand that
hasn't arrived yet."

"How on earth are we to know?" said Peter. "The

mean pig hasn't brought us a present, and I'm hanged if he shall carry one off."

"Tomorrow, when he's having his bath," said Mrs. Peter excitedly, "he's sure to leave his keys somewhere, and we can go through his portmanteau. It's the only thing to do."

On the morrow an alert watch was kept by the conspirators behind half-closed doors, and when Wilfrid, clad in a gorgeous bathrobe, had made his way to the bathroom, there was a swift and furtive rush by two excited individuals towards the principal guestchamber. Mrs. Peter kept guard outside, while her husband first made a hurried and successful search for the keys, and then plunged at the portmanteau with the air of a disagreeably conscientious customs official. The quest was a brief one; a silver cream jug lay embedded in the folds of some zephyr shirts.

"The cunning brute," said Mrs. Peter; "he took a cream jug because there were so many; he thought one wouldn't be missed. Quick, fly down with it and put it back among the others."

Wilfrid was late in coming down to breakfast, and his manner showed plainly that something was amiss.

"It's an unpleasant thing to have to say," he blurted out presently, "but I'm afraid you must have a thief among your servants. Something's been taken out of my portmanteau. It was a little present from my mother and myself for your silver wedding. I should have given it to you last night after dinner, only it happened to be a cream jug, and you seemed annoyed at having so many duplicates, so I felt rather awkward about giving you another. I thought I'd get it changed for something else, and now it's gone."

"Did you say it was from your *mother* and yourself?" asked Mr. and Mrs. Peter almost in unison. The Snatcher had been an orphan these many years.

"Yes, my mother's at Cairo just now, and she wrote to me at Dresden to try and get you something quaint and pretty in the old silver line, and I pitched on this cream jug."

Both the Pigeoncotes had turned deadly pale. The mention of Dresden had thrown a sudden light on the situation. It was Wilfrid the Attaché, a very superior young man, who rarely came within their social horizon, whom they had been entertaining unawares in the supposed character of Wilfrid the Snatcher. Lady Ernestine Pigeoncote, his mother, moved in circles which were entirely beyond their compass or ambitions, and the son would probably one day be an ambassador. And they had rifled and despoiled his portmanteau! Husband and wife looked blankly and desperately at one another. It was Mrs. Peter who arrived first at an inspiration.

"How dreadful to think there are thieves in the house! We keep the drawing room locked up at night, of course, but anything might be carried off while we are at breakfast."

She rose and went out hurriedly, as though to assure herself that the drawing room was not being stripped of its silverware, and returned a moment later, bearing a cream jug in her hands.

"There are eight cream jugs now, instead of seven," she cried; "this one wasn't there before. What a curious trick of memory, Mr. Wilfrid! You must have slipped downstairs with it last night and put it there before we locked up, and forgotten all about having done it in the morning."

"One's mind often plays one little tricks like that," said Mr. Peter, with desperate heartiness. "Only the other day I went into the town to pay a bill, and went in again next day, having clean forgotten that I'd—"

"It is certainly the jug that I brought for you," said Wilfrid, looking closely at it; "it was in my portmanteau when I got my bathrobe out this morning, before going to my bath, and it was not there when I unlocked the portmanteau on my return. Someone had taken it while I was away from the room."

The Pigeoncotes had turned paler than ever. Mrs. Peter had a final inspiration.

"Get me my smelling salts, dear," she said to her husband; "I think they're in the dressing room."

Peter dashed out of the room with glad relief; he had lived so long during the last few minutes that a golden wedding seemed within measurable distance.

Mrs. Peter turned to her guest with confidential coyness.

"A diplomat like you will know how to treat this as if it hadn't happened. Peter's little weakness; it runs in the family."

"Good Lord! Do you mean to say he's a kleptomaniac, like Cousin Snatcher?"

"Oh, not exactly," said Mrs. Peter, anxious to whitewash her husband a little greyer than she was painting him. "He would never touch anything he found lying about, but he can't resist making a raid on things that are locked up. The doctors have a special name for it. He must have pounced on your portmanteau the moment you went to your bath, and taken the first thing he came across. Of course, he had no motive for taking a cream jug; we've already got *seven*, as you know—not, of course, that we don't value the kind gift you and your mother—— Hush, here's Peter coming."

Mrs. Peter broke off in some confusion, and tripped out to meet her husband in the hall.

"It's all right," she whispered to him; "I've explained everything. Don't say anything more about it."

"Brave little woman," said Peter, with a gasp of relief; "I could never have done it."

Diplomatic reticence does not necessarily extend to family affairs. Peter Pigeoncote was never able to understand why Mrs. Consuelo van Bullyon, who stayed with them in the spring, always carried two very obvious jewel cases with her to the bathroom, explaining them to anyone she chanced to meet in the corridor as her manicure and face-massage set.

The Gala Programme

An Unrecorded Episode in Roman History

IT WAS an auspicious day in the Roman Calendar, the birthday of the popular and gifted young Emperor Placidus Superbus. Everyone in Rome was bent on keeping high festival, the weather was at its best, and naturally the Imperial Circus was crowded to its fullest capacity. A few minutes before the hour fixed for the commencement of the spectacle a loud fanfare of trumpets proclaimed the arrival of Caesar, and amid the vociferous acclamations of the multitude the Emperor took his seat in the Imperial Box. As the shouting of the crowd died away an even more thrilling salutation could be heard in the near distance, the angry, impatient roaring and howling of the beasts caged in the Imperial menagerie.

"Explain the programme to me," commanded the Emperor, having beckoned the Master of the Ceremonies to his side.

That eminent official wore a troubled look.

"Gracious Caesar," he announced, "a most promising and entertaining programme has been devised and prepared for your august approval. In the first place there is to be a chariot contest of unusual brilliancy and interest; three teams that have

152

never hitherto suffered defeat are to contend for the
Herculaneum Trophy, together with the purse which
your Imperial generosity has been pleased to add.
The chances of the competing teams are accounted
to be as nearly as possible equal, and there is much
wagering among the populace. The black Thracians
are perhaps the favourites——"

"I know, I know," interrupted Caesar, who had
listened to exhaustive talk on the same subject all the
morning; "what else is there on the programme?"

"The second part of the programme," said the Imperial Official, "consists of a grand combat of wild
beasts, specially selected for their strength, ferocity,
and fighting qualities. There will appear simulta-
neously in the arena fourteen Nubian lions and lion-
esses, five tigers, six Syrian bears, eight Persian pan-
thers, and three North African ditto, a number of
wolves and lynxes from the Teutonic forests, and
seven gigantic wild bulls from the same region.
There will also be wild swine of unexampled savage-
ness, a rhinoceros from the Barbary coast, some fe-
rocious man-apes, and a hyena, reputed to be mad."

"It promises well," said the Emperor.

"It *promised* well, O Caesar," said the official
dolorously, "it promised marvellously well; but between the promise and the performance a cloud has
arisen."

"A cloud? What cloud?" queried Caesar, with a
frown.

"The Suffragetae," explained the official; "they
threaten to interfere with the chariot race."

"I'd like to see them do it!" exclaimed the Emperor
indignantly.

"I fear your Impèrial wish may be unpleasantly

gratified," said the Master of the Ceremonies; "we are taking, of course, every possible precaution, and guarding all the entrances to the arena and the stables with a triple guard; but it is rumoured that at the signal for the entry of the chariots five hundred women will let themselves down with ropes from the public seats and swarm all over the course. Naturally no race could be run under such circumstances; the programme will be ruined.

"On my birthday," said Placidus Superbus, "they would not dare to do such an outrageous thing."

"The more august the occasion, the more desirous they will be to advertise themselves and their cause," said the harassed official; "they do not scruple to make riotous interference even with the ceremonies in the temples."

"Who *are* these Suffragetae?" asked the Emperor. "Since I came back from my Pannonian expedition I have heard of nothing else but their excesses and demonstrations."

"They are a political sect of very recent origin, and their aim seems to be to get a big share of political authority into their hands. The means they are taking to convince us of their fitness to help in making and administering the laws consist of wild indulgence in tumult, destruction, and defiance of all authority. They have already damaged some of the most historically valuable of our public treasures, which can never be replaced."

"Is it possible that the sex which we hold in such honour and for which we feel such admiration can produce such hordes of Furies?" asked the Emperor.

"It takes all sorts to make a sex," observed the Master of Ceremonies, who possessed a certain amount of worldly wisdom; "also," he continued anxiously, "it takes very little to upset a gala programme."

"Perhaps the disturbance that you anticipate will turn out to be an idle threat," said the Emperor consolingly.

"But if they should carry out their intention," said the official, "the programme will be utterly ruined."

The Emperor said nothing.

Five minutes later the trumpets rang out for the commencement of the entertainment. A hum of excited anticipation ran through the ranks of the spectators, and final bets on the issue of the great race were hurriedly shouted. The gates leading from the stables were slowly swung open, and a troop of mounted attendants rode round the track to ascertain that everything was clear for the momentous contest. Again the trumpets rang out, and then, before the foremost chariot had appeared, there arose a wild tumult of shouting, laughing, angry protests, and shrill screams of defiance. Hundreds of women were being lowered by their accomplices into the arena. A moment later they were running and dancing in frenzied troops across the track where the chariots were supposed to compete. No team of arena-trained horses would have faced such a frantic mob; the race was clearly an impossibility. Howls of disappointment and rage rose from the spectators, howls of triumph echoed back from the women in possession. The vain efforts of the circus attendants to drive out the invading horde merely added to the uproar and confusion; as fast as the Suffragetae were thrust away from one portion of the track they swarmed onto another.

The Master of the Ceremonies was nearly delirious from rage and mortification.

Placidus Superbus, who remained calm, and unruffled as ever, beckoned to him and spoke a word or two in his ear. For the first time that afternoon the sorely tried official was seen to smile.

A trumpet rang out from the Imperial Box; an instant hush fell over the excited throng. Perhaps the Emperor, as a last resort, was going to announce some concession to the Suffragetae.

"Close the stable gates," commanded the Master of the Ceremonies, "and open all the menagerie dens. It is the Imperial pleasure that the second portion of the programme be taken first."

It turned out that the Master of the Ceremonies had in no wise exaggerated the probable brilliancy of this portion of the spectacle. The wild bulls were really wild, and the hyena reputed to be mad thoroughly lived up to its reputation.